R.N.F. (RICHARD) SKINNER i
a writer by inclination, and a me
for remuneration. He has publisl
(as Richard Skinner), and two
Crazy... (SilverWood 2020), and
comedy sketches, After All... ('

composed lyrics for a range of songs including the Christmas
musical *Bethlehem!*

While an undergraduate at Cambridge University, as well
as being a member of the famous *Footlights* club, he co-founded
and performed extensively with the cabaret-revue team Seventh
Sense. He continues occasionally to write and perform sketch-
based comedy.

Though a Londoner by upbringing, he has lived in Exeter
for many years. He has qualified as a social worker, and in 2012
he was awarded a doctorate from Exeter University for his thesis
on religion and evolutionary theory. He lives with his wife, three
hens, a dog and a cat.

For further information about his books please visit his
website at rnfskinner.com or contact him at richardskinner.
exeter@gmail.com

Also by R N F Skinner

Fiction
Still Crazy… (SilverWood 2020)
After All… (SilverWood 2022)

Poetry (as Richard Skinner)
Leaping & Staggering (Dilettante 1988/1996)
In the Stillness: based on Julian of Norwich (Dilettante 1990/2013)
The Melting Woman (Blue Button 1993)
Still Staggering (Dilettante 1995)
Echoes of Eckhart (Cairns/Arthur James 1998)
The Logic of Whistling (Cairns 2002)
Invocations (Wild Goose 2005)
Colliding With God (Wild Goose 2016)
A brief poetry of time (Oversteps 2017)
The Colour of Water (Dilettante 2023)

THESE YEARS:
1973

R.N.F. SKINNER

SilverWood

Published in 2024 by SilverWood Books

SilverWood Books Ltd
14 Small Street, Bristol, BS1 1DE, United Kingdom
www.silverwoodbooks.co.uk

ISBN 978-1-80042-275-9 (paperback)
Also available as an ebook

British Library Cataloguing in Publication Data
A CIP catalogue record for this book is
available from the British Library

Page design and typesetting by SilverWood Books

For Betsy

Acknowledgements

Many thanks to David Thompson for his suggestion that I develop the original short story into a considerably longer piece; to Lesley Hart, the freelance fiction editor at Author's Pen (authorspen.co.uk), whose expertise has been brilliant; to Helen Hart for managing to combine the friendliest of approaches with the highest of publishing standards at SilverWood; and, as ever, to my wife Betsy for her unflagging love, support and encouragement for my varied writing projects.

i

In a modest grey brick house, its frontage partially covered in wisteria not yet in bloom, situated on the outskirts of North Adams in the north-west corner of Massachusetts, Ruth Whitehead, twelve years old for a few more weeks, was sitting in front of her bedroom mirror late one afternoon in March, sullenly brushing her long mousy brown hair. Her mom had told her to tidy her room before they all went out and thankfully hair-brushing delayed that task.

But yes, she had to admit her room looked even messier than usual, the trouble being, as she had often thought, that although sizable, it wasn't quite big enough for all her furniture and other things: this dressing table, dominated by its silvery-framed but speckled oval mirror, given to her when Nana had died; the wooden-framed bed, currently hosting a scatter of clothes, more of which lay strewn across the floor; two floor-to-ceiling cupboards decorated with a jungle motif in hand-painted luxuriant and colourful growth, doors wide open, clutter spilling out; a squat and cumbersome chest of drawers covered with a red-and-gold patterned cloth across which an entire menagerie of little glass animals roamed. Next to it, a glass-fronted bookcase with paperbacks and a few hardbacks all higgledy-piggledy except for one proper row of books in size order with *sketching*, *drawing* or *painting* in their titles; and under the window, most important of all as far as she was concerned, stood a stout wooden bench, which her dad had constructed, where she kept her sketching materials all neatly laid out: pads of cartridge paper, pencils, pencil sharpeners, erasers, charcoal sticks in a flat tin, and some stubs of very superior oil-sticks, which her art teacher, Miss Abrams, had passed on to her. Her current sketch-in-progress, of a fluffy cat with a flattish face – probably Persian, Mom had told her – stretched out along the branch of a tree, occupied the centre of the table. Several other sketches and drawings, and a couple of her paintings including a vivid depiction of Walden Pond in the fall, adorned the bedroom walls, along with a collage of David Cassidy, her current favourite heartthrob. She had created the collage only three or four weeks previously out of pictures and slogans cut from back issues of *Tiger Beat*.

She had been counting the brush strokes under her breath, and now she announced out loud, "Ninety-eight, ninety-nine, a hundred!" and banged the brush down on the dressing table. That was that done. Not that it had improved her hair – tidier, she supposed, but that didn't stop it being dry and dull. She wished it were blonde and shiny. Like Donna's. Everyone says how *lovely* Donna's hair is, usually while saying how *pretty* Donna is and how *cute* she is. Sometimes Ruth wonders if she actually hates Donna even though Donna is her very best friend, most of the time at least, and she honestly *is* both pretty and cute. But no, she couldn't hate Donna at all, not really, but she felt – what? Jealous? Envious? Never quite sure of the difference, Ruth reverted to just wishing her hair were the twin of Donna's.

She did not really want to go out that evening to her aunt and uncle's, where they were to meet Mom's and Aunt Lou's cousin-in-law or whatever he was from England. Cousin Greg, as she'd been told to call him.

Uncle Harold had already shown her a complicated diagram of family relationships he had drawn up, full of little circles and squares with names by them and notes in his tiny handwriting, all connected by lots of horizontal and vertical lines showing how everyone was related to everyone else through births and marriages and remarriages over many generations. She was there, naturally, at the lowest level, along with her cousins Edward and Bradley, known to everyone as Ted and Brad. The boys were squares, but she, being a girl, was a circle, and a solitary circle at that, annotated with the information: Ruth Louise, b. 5/18/1960.

Tracing connections through the network with his finger, Uncle Harold had explained exactly why she and Cousin Greg, although not actual straight-forward cousins, were third – or was it fourth? – cousins something or other removed. He said it was probably easiest to think of Cousin Greg simply as a distant relative.

Why couldn't Cousin Greg have *stayed* distant? she grumbled to herself, still sitting gazing into the mirror full of reflections of multiple David Cassidys. If this cousin had to come to the States for some wedding or whatever it was in New York, why couldn't he have stayed on there or just gone straight back to England when it was over? Why come here? She certainly didn't want to meet him.

But she knew the real reason for not wanting to go to her aunt and uncle's was Brad. Brad, now fifteen, had taken to teasing her. Teasing her a lot. His teasing had always been friendly before, but had now become quite mocking and hurtful. Especially the way he kept referring to her as Ruth-*less*. Even though on two or three occasions he had tried to kiss her. She had had to push him away, saying crossly, "Get *off*!"

"I think he's missing his brother," Mom had said by way of explanation.

This puzzled Ruth. "Does he kiss Ted, then?"

Hands on hips, Mom gave her a look. "It's why he's generally annoying."

"Oh. But it's not my fault Ted's gone to college."

"I know, honey," hands off hips, "but I guess without having Ted around to look up to, Brad's feeling a bit lost."

Recalling one of Donna's favourite remarks, Ruth wished Brad would *get* lost, but didn't say so.

"I'll have a word with Aunt Lou if you like?" Mom continued.

Ruth shook her head. "It's okay. I don't want to tell tales out of school."

"As you wish, honey. Just as long as you're all right about it. I'm sure he'll get over it soon. He's at an awkward age."

But that had been in the fall, months ago, and Brad's age, it would seem, continued to be awkward.

She gazed into the mirror. It was difficult to tell, but she was sure its speckles made her face look even more freckled. She bared her teeth, examining her brace. How much longer would she have to wear it? Since getting it, she had tried to create a smile that looked pretty, cute and winning without revealing the brace, but all her attempts made her look, well, just stupid. She'd resorted to putting her hand up to her mouth when speaking, only her parents and teachers complained they couldn't hear her properly. She bet if Donna had a brace – which she didn't – she'd smile gaily, show off the brace as though it were a rare piece of jewellery, and be thought even more cute.

At least she had clothes she liked – Mom had bought her dress, pale yellow with puffed sleeves, and on her last birthday Aunt Lou had given her the two silvery metal bangles, inscribed with tiny animal faces, saying that as she and Uncle Harold had only sons, Ruth should have the bangles, which Aunt Lou herself had worn as a young woman. They were really neat, but she had to be careful as they were just slightly too large and would slip off her wrists if she weren't careful. Not that she wanted her wrists any thicker. She still hadn't acted on Mom's suggestion of wearing a third, slightly tighter bangle to secure the other two.

She stood up, twirled around and came to a stop, holding out the hem of the dress and curtseying to the Partridge Family pop star.

She knew she ought to get on with the tidying up, but the cat-in-the-tree sketch was calling her. Several of the large, lower branches of the tree, a great white oak with light grey bark near her school, grew out almost horizontally, and the cat would sprawl along one spectacularly rough and rugged branch, its tail dangling down as if to tease boys in particular by being just out of reach. Donna had suggested it would be a good subject for the annual local art competition Ruth wanted to enter.

"You'll walk it," Donna had said, giving her slinky walk impression of a fashion model on a catwalk. "You're *sooo* good. Miss Abrams thinks so too."

Ruth sat at the table, frowning. Something had been bothering her about the sketch, and she now realized what needed altering. She picked up an eraser, and then the BB pencil.

ii

Ruth's uncle and aunt's red brick house, larger than her own home, often referred to as *the mansion* by the family, had rather severe rectangular windows, two on either side of the elaborate porch with its tall columns surmounted by a squashed-looking pediment, and a row of five more rectangular windows along the upper storey. No wisteria or any other climbing plant softened its façade, which, Ruth had long since discovered, made it much less interesting to draw.

As they turned into the drive, she saw Uncle Harold's car, a large black vehicle he called his *tank*, standing in the carport between his workshop and the house. Mom tutted in annoyance. "We should have got here earlier, Harold's already collected him. The bus must have got in early."

"No matter," Dad murmured, parking their more modest car next to Aunt Lou's little red runabout beside the carport. "As long as he's arrived." Clutching at his old-fashioned fedora, which he even wore in the car, he got out and hurried round to hold open the passenger door for his wife. She struggled out, for though slight in physique she often moved with apparent difficulty as if ill at ease.

"Hi, folks!" Ruth's uncle called out as she too scrambled from the car. Quite a lot shorter than Dad, Uncle Harold was clean-shaven – in a way resembling his house, Ruth had often thought, with his glasses as windows, whereas Dad with his straggly beard matched their house with its untamed wisteria. Her uncle was walking rapidly towards them with his abbreviated clip-clopping tread, right arm held stiffly away from his body as though it were a rudder to help him steer through the light rain, which had been falling intermittently all day. Ruth gave a brief smile, reminded of Donna's comment that, "Your uncle walks like he needs to get to the bathroom before he has an accident!"

"Come on, folks, come on!" He briefly kissed his sister-in-law on the cheek, patted Ruth on the head in the way she particularly disliked, and slapped her dad on the back, nearly dislodging the fedora.

"Careful now, Harold," Dad warned. "Mind m'Gandhi." He always referred to whatever hat he was wearing as 'm'Gandhi', explaining, whenever asked, that he named all his headgear after Mahatma Gandhi, before usually having to elaborate: "my hat, m'Gandhi." He frequently made jokey comments that Ruth usually didn't understand, and other people usually didn't laugh at. Some of his lines he took from *Reader's Digest*; the positioning of its apostrophe, he claimed, implied that it had only one reader, which must be him.

Brad sauntered out of the house, jerking his head to flick his long fair hair away from his face. He had one hand plunged into the pocket of a bulky brown jacket Ruth had not seen him in before. Its broad expanse of collar had a sheepskin lining. "Cool, eh?" He opened the jacket, displaying the rest of the lining. "It's Greg's bomber jacket."

"What does that mean?"

"It means that guys in the war in bomber planes wore jackets like this to keep them warm."

"Was he in the war, then?"

"No! 'Course not," in that sarcastic tone he had recently adopted. "He's twenty-two, Dad said, not old enough. But it's real neat, isn't it."

"Real neat," she agreed unenthusiastically as they all headed indoors.

Aunt Lou, bright-eyed and bosomy, abundant fair but greying hair newly styled with curly wisps dangling down, was waiting in the largest of the downstairs rooms, along with the visitor, who stood up as they entered. Ruth quickly took him in. Tall, taller even than Dad, and slightly round-shouldered. Untidy brown hair covering his ears. So this was Cousin Greg? Big deal, she thought.

"Here they are," Aunt Lou said to him. "This is my sister, Nancy."

"Hi, Nancy, good to meet you!" Holding out a hand, he smiled a lopsided smile as though a fishhook had snagged the left-hand side of his top lip and was tugging it upwards. "I'm Greg, as I guess you'll have guessed!"

"Welcome to Massachusetts, Greg."

"And, er, George."

"Hi, George." More handshaking. "Good to meet you."

"And you, young man."

"And Ruth, their daughter Ruth, my lovely niece!" Aunt Lou put a gentle arm round Ruth's shoulders.

"Yeah?" Greg again smiling lopsidedly, briefly waving a hand at her instead of offering it to be shaken. "Hi, Ruth. Great to see you. This is quite a welcoming committee, yeah?"

Ruth gave a tiny reluctant wave in return. Her cousin's denims were scruffier than she or Brad would be allowed to wear. His blue sweatshirt had a white stripe round the neck. And although his sneakers looked new, Ruth got the impression he wasn't too bothered about clothes.

"Take a seat, everyone," Aunt Lou said cheerfully, spreading her hands to indicate the two deep, comfortable sofas and matching armchairs you could practically disappear into, their cushions ready plumped. "The kettle's on, and there's cake to keep us going until dinner."

"Can I help?" Ruth, still feeling irritated at having to be there, didn't sit down.

"Of course you can, poppet." Aunt Lou, who always seemed to understand her, bustled away towards the kitchen. "That'd be lovely."

*

Ruth felt a yawn coming – being made to listen to their conversation was all so boring. How was the flight, Greg? How are your parents keeping, Greg? What's the weather like in England at the moment, Greg? Then Greg had asked Uncle Harold what his line of business was, and there had followed a long explanation about *AirConPro*, the company he and Dad had set up, all to do with fans and air conditioning and dull stuff like that. She had heard it all before, how Uncle Harold headed up the design department, how Dad saw to the finance and marketing.

"I always wish," Dad broke into his business partner's monologue, "that we'd called the firm *Thank You*."

"Why's that?" Greg was rubbing his chin, his hand making a faint rasping sound against his stubble.

"Because then we could have as the firm's motto, *Thank You Fans*."

Why did Dad make these silly comments? Ruth felt a twinge of embarrassment. She had heard this one so many times before. But Greg threw his head back as though he were a performing

17

seal, and gave a series of brief, barking laughs in a descending scale.

Then more dull stuff as Mom took the opportunity to change the subject, asking in what Ruth thought of as her giving-you-the-third-degree voice, "How did the wedding go, Greg?" She patted her hair, which was springy and would not remain flat. She had recently developed this habit of touching her dark mop of hair, which Ruth thought was like someone with a wig making sure it hadn't slipped or blown off. "You were best man, weren't you? In New York?"

"Yeah, that's right." Greg stretched out his legs. Sprawled in one of the armchairs in the way that would get Ruth told by her mom to sit up properly, you'll get round-shouldered, he didn't seem to have noticed that the lace of one of his sneakers had come loose. "It went fine, thanks, Nancy. Scarsdale, actually. Then I got to see a bit of the Big Apple for a couple of days."

Brad, still wearing the bomber jacket, also stretched out his legs. Was he, Ruth wondered, deliberately copying Cousin Greg? He had a look of fierce concentration on his face.

"Scarsdale? Very swanky!" Dad was chuckling.

"You're telling me, George. I'm not sure Chris knew what he was letting himself in for, marrying a Stateside girl!"

Ruth's yawn broke through, but she managed to convert it into more of a nervous gasp, blurting out, "Who's Chris?"

"An old school friend, Ruth. We live in neighbouring villages in Devon, if you know where that is. South-west bit of England. He's a fellow artist."

A fellow artist? Feeling herself flush, Ruth quickly looked away, enjoying a sensation of unexpected pleasure. She turned back. "Are you an artist, then?"

"Guilty as charged." He smiled lopsidedly at her.

"Well now, that's something we have in common." Uncle Harold pointed at a framed drawing on the wall. "That's the design I drew up in '55 of the variable-speed mark two extractor with the optimized twin flow option. Our very first success story. I pride myself on my technical drawings."

"You do indeed, Harold," Dad said in his quiet way. "But I don't suppose that's quite what Greg does. Or is it?" he appealed to the visitor.

"Not exactly, but it's very impressive. Meticulous." Greg nodded several times, evidently at a loss.

"It's Harold's forte." Dad was tugging on his beard, looking like an ancient Chinese philosopher dispensing wisdom. He was, Ruth thought, nothing like pushy enough in dealing with her uncle, who always seemed to think other people ought to be interested in everything *he* was interested in.

"What got you into it, Greg?" Aunt Lou asked. She always sounded interested in other people. "Doing art, I mean?"

"I never really wanted to do anything else," he said, clasping his hands behind his head. "I was always painting, sketching, drawing. Drove my teachers mad, but I was useful for them as well – posters for school plays and...you know." He became more animated. "I love doing publicity posters, great fun. A couple of friends, Phil and Rob, put on comedy shows, so I do their publicity. Oh, and for a theatre chap, James Tredwell. 'Tredders' to all and sundry. Completely bonkers. Yeah, I like doing posters and things like that, but principally I'm a painter."

"What sort of things do you paint?" Ruth asked quickly before anyone else could speak. She simply had to hear more. "Do you do abstracts or repersent...reprents..." She stumbled to a halt, mortified at hearing Brad snigger.

"Both," Greg said, unclasping his hands and leaning forward, "but mainly repersent... Ha! You've got me at it now. Tricky word. Representational! I particularly like portraits, but I've recently done a commission for a children's picture book. My main subjects usually come from the natural world—"

"Mine too," Ruth interrupted breathlessly. "I like drawing trees and flowers. And painting them. What do you—"

"Don't quiz the poor man," Mom interrupted in turn. Feeling abashed, Ruth fell silent.

"It's okay, Nancy." Greg held up a hand. "I don't mind. In fact, I rather like talking about it. So, you're an artist as well, are you, Ruth? That's great. We must talk painting and stuff some time. How about you, Brad?" He turned to her cousin. "Are you into art? Or something else?"

As Brad shrugged, Uncle Harold answered for him. "He's a great sports player. Loves his soccer, don't you? Supports your Manchester team."

"United," Brad grunted. "Not City."

"Good choice," Greg said without sounding very enthusiastic.

Although the conversation had already veered away from art, its very mention had changed everything for Ruth. Unable to sit still, she got up, muttering that she was going to the bathroom, and left the room. One of the few specific things she remembered from tedious church services was Pastor Gravatt reading and then talking for ages about a passage from the Bible where St Paul is suddenly converted when he's on his way to somewhere and being made blind. Well, she hadn't gone blind – she peered at her reflection in the bathroom mirror to reassure herself – but all the same everything about Cousin Greg had totally changed in a kind of blinding flash. He was an *artist*.

When she returned to the main room, Uncle Harold was saying, "…enjoy yourself while you're here. It's good to have the English side of the family represented. Though mind you," he gave a conspiratorial chuckle, "Lou and Nancy's ancestors might have hailed originally from Scotland, och aye the noo!"

An inexplicable collective chuckling sounded from the adults.

"If their family legend is to be believed," Uncle Harold continued, "there's a McIver ancestor in the mix who, shall we say, appears to have enjoyed the favours of an English *maid*." Ruth could hear inverted commas.

More collective chuckling.

"He had what's known as a highland fling—" her dad began.

"George!" Mom spoke sharply, giving a little shake of her head. Aunt Lou was smiling indulgently.

Ruth was feeling left out. "What's a highland fling?"

"It's a particular way of dancing in Scotland." Greg turned to her. "That's all I know about it, though."

"Thank you, Greg," Mom said in a relieved tone.

Brad was smirking, and Ruth's sense of being excluded deepened. "How *are* we related, though? If we're distant relatives or something."

"Good question," Greg agreed. "My mother did try explaining when she suggested I come on up here after the wedding to say hi to my transatlantic relatives, but she got in a right muddle."

"I'll show you the official family tree," Uncle Harold said eagerly, getting to his feet.

"No need for that, Harold," Aunt Lou said quickly. "As you know," she looked round at the others, "once he gets started, he never stops. Quite simply, Greg," she continued as Uncle Harold

21

subsided back into his chair, "our great-great-grandfather, that's Nancy's and mine, lived in Liverpool – that's in the north of England," she explained to everyone else. "And he was *English*."

Aunt Lou continued to explain, but Ruth lost track when it came to Greg's great-great-grandmother's second husband's first wife. Or something. How wonderful, though, she was thinking, that Cousin Greg calls her parents George and Nancy, not Mr and Mrs Whitehead. And her uncle and aunt are simply Harold and Lou to him, not Mr and Mrs Watson. She realizes how much she loves his voice – his accent, the casual way he speaks, his use of 'yeah' – and the way he sprawls in his chair. That's because he's an *artist*. Has he brought anything of his with him? Could she show him some of her sketches? Her paintings? Could she risk it? Surely he'd be kind – his stumble over that word hadn't fooled her; obviously he really knew how to pronounce it. He was just being thoughtful...

As the explanation of how everyone was related to everyone else unfolded, Uncle Harold having corrected Aunt Lou about some great-great-aunt or other, Ruth could see that Greg was listening with the look she knew she had when she'd lost all interest in something. Eyes unfocussed, lips twitching slightly. Suddenly he started waggling one of his feet. His legs were crossed at the ankles, and the top foot, his right one, had taken on a life of its own. Backwards and forwards it went, up and down, then describing part of a circle, then back again. As Uncle Harold droned on, Greg's foot-waggling increased, like someone more and more impatiently rattling the handle of a locked door, until he abruptly uncrossed his legs, crossed them again the other way round, and started foot-waggling with his left foot, which made the loose shoelace untie itself completely.

Ruth felt a giggle rising up. She opened her eyes wide and bit her lip, then put her hand up to hide her brace as she tried to breathe steadily through her open mouth to suppress the insistent giggle. Now Brad, legs still stretched out, had started foot-waggling in unison; Greg noticed, looked at his own foot, and drew both his feet in. The giggle pressure subsided.

"You see, Ruth," Greg raised a hand to interrupt Uncle Harold in mid-flow, which she had never known anyone else being able to do, "that's why we're definitely distant relatives!"

"But we're not distant relatives anymore, are we?" she said excitedly, lowering her hand and exposing the dental brace. "You and me."

A brief silence, broken by a snort from Brad.

"What do you mean, honey?" Mom quizzed her.

"Because Greg's here now, isn't he?"

"*Cousin* Greg," Mom corrected.

"No, no!" Greg said. "That's okay. You call me Greg, Ruth; everyone else does. It's my name! Yeah?"

"Yeah," Ruth echoed faintly.

"And I'm not really your cousin in any case. Not like you and Brad are."

Brad scowled.

"You and I are something like fifty-eighth cousins twenty-three times removed," Greg continued, "or whatever Harold was saying. So, we're very, *very* distant relatives!"

Ruth saw her uncle stiffen as though he had been insulted by Cousin Greg's flippancy – no, *Greg's* flippancy.

"But you're here now," Ruth repeated to Greg. "England's a long way away so you're distant when you're there, but now you're here you're very close…" Her voice tailed away as she realized that Brad was again smirking and the adults – other than Greg himself – were once more chuckling.

"Ruthless the Dumbo," Brad said. "*Distant relative* doesn't mean how far apart you are in miles or anything like that—"

"Brad!" Aunt Lou gave a quiet warning.

"What does it mean, then?" Ruth asked.

As Brad, ignoring his mother, started to spell it out, Ruth felt misery engulf her. How *stupid* she had been. But Greg's voice rose above Brad's, silencing it and rescuing her.

"Hey, hey, hey!" tapping an arm of his chair three or four times. "I get what Ruth means, and she's right. This distant relative stuff about who's related to who is all very well, but it's just great to meet different people, whether or not we're related in any special way. But Ruth's dead right. Two weeks ago, I was three thousand miles away or whatever, yeah? Which is definitely distant. But now I'm about what? Three *feet* away. Yeah? Definitely not distant!" He looked at her and nodded. "You're right, Ruth, we *are* close relatives at the moment! Hey, Lou, no more cake, thanks," as she held out the plate to him, "but I wouldn't say no to more tea. We English like our tea, yeah?"

As fresh tea was being fetched, Ruth – leaning forward, hands clasping her knees, not caring that she must be madly blushing, not caring about the brace on her teeth, not caring about Mom frowning at her and Brad scowling and Dad with his faraway look and Uncle Harold cleaning his glasses with a handkerchief – asked Greg all about the book he was illustrating.

iii

"*And* he's an artist," Ruth said with a degree of possessive pride. "Some of his paintings are going to be illustrations in a children's book. An adventure story about a boy and his horse who go on a long journey and have these adventures. He's going to be famous!"

Donna looked suitably impressed. "That's so *cool*," she declared authoritatively. "A real live artist? Have you seen any of the pictures?"

"N-no," Ruth conceded. "He hasn't got those ones with him but," trying not to sound as though she were boasting, "he'd like to show me some of the things he draws. His sketches."

There were still a few minutes to go before they were due in school, and the two girls were sitting on a wooden bench on the expanse of grass opposite with its trees and flowerbeds, beneath the particular tree where the fluffy grey cat often occupied a branch. He wasn't there that morning.

"He's going to bring his sketch pad when they all come over this evening," Ruth continued. "I asked him if he would and he said he'd like to, but he didn't want to bore anyone, and I said *I* wouldn't be bored, I'd be really interested because I like drawing. So, he's going to show me," she finished in a rush.

"He's going to show you? Oooh!" Donna said knowingly, kicking out her legs, her regulation green skirt, which she wore with an inch or so rolled-up at the waist, barely long enough to satisfy the school authorities. Three months older than Ruth, she could be rather more, with signs of puberty developing, and a tendency to find meanings in innocent remarks that Ruth didn't always understand. "Are you going to show him anything?" she asked, having finished her Oooh-ing. "I think you should, you know. You could show him that picture Miss Abrams gave you a gold star for last week, those wildflowers. It's really good."

"I don't know." Ruth thrust out her lower lip. "D'you think I should? Suppose he thinks it's awful? He might – he's a *proper* artist. Miss Abrams isn't, not really. Maybe I'll only show him something if he asks? He might not want to."

"Of course he'll want to! I bet he'll be pleased. And he's not going to think that anything you draw is awful! I know!" Donna clapped in excitement. "I could come round as well and show him some of the drawings I've done – now they *are* awful! Then you show him yours! Da-dah! Genius! He'll fall in love with you there and then when he sees how good you are at drawing! You'll have to take down those David Cassidy pictures, though!" And she started singing 'Could It Be Forever'.

"Stop it!" Ruth slapped her friend on the arm, though feeling pleasure at the idea. "He won't fall in love with me! Any more than David Cassidy will!"

Despite the slap, Donna had continued singing. Now she broke off mid-verse. "More chance! David Cassidy has no idea who you are! But anyway," dramatically placing a hand on her heart, "if Greg doesn't fall in love with you, he can fall in love with me instead!"

When Ruth had started telling Donna about the previous evening, her friend had sighed at her description of Greg being *so* good-looking, and sniggered at Ruth's account of him smiling at her. And now she was suggesting Greg might even fall in love with her. Or with Donna herself, which would be *far* more likely.

Or would it? He might fall in love with me, Ruth thought, mightn't he? He might see past her annoying hair and the brace on her teeth and her skinny body and her freckles, and fall in love with her as a budding artist. But then again, she was only twelve and Greg was what? Twenty-two, Brad had said, and he was bound to have a girlfriend already. Or lots of girlfriends probably because artists always have lots of girlfriends. Or boyfriends. Did that mean she would have lots of boyfriends when she was older? She sighed. Not very likely. The fact was that she *did* have annoying hair and freckles and *was* skinny, however good she might be at drawing. Donna, on the other hand, would be the one to have lots of boyfriends when she grew up, even though she couldn't draw for toffee. In fact, Donna already had older boys wanting to date her and she kept telling them to get lost.

*

Whether or not Greg could possibly fall in love with her, Ruth had already decided she wouldn't be telling Donna how the evening had ended. For when the time had come to leave, she had, as usual, kissed her aunt and uncle goodbye – but not Brad, who had, to her relief, already disappeared into his room – and then she had hesitated awkwardly in front of Greg. Standing, he gazed down at her from an Olympian height. She put out her hand to shake his.

"Hey, hey, hey!" Greg had said, leaning down. "I thought we were close relatives now!" And he had kissed her on the cheek, his bristles feeling strange against her face, adding, "Goodnight, Ruthie!" to her and her parents as he straightened up. "See you lot tomorrow evening! Yeah?"

Ruth echoed, "Yeah," and saw Mom frown at her as Uncle Harold confirmed, "That's the plan. We're all coming over to you."

Ruth had been in a dream during the car ride home. Greg had kissed her. Kissed *her*. Greg had *kissed* HER. He had called her Ruthie and kissed her. And when she was curled up in bed, she had imagined herself kissing him, which she had then practised by kissing her pillow several times.

*

"Are you two comin' in?" A familiar voice brought Ruth back to the school day. Jasmine, her other good school friend, was standing in front of her and Donna, holding out a hand to each. Ruth jumped up. So lucky to have friends like Donna, a blonde bombshell in the making, as Dad had put it, and Jasmine, a young Tina Turner lookalike, with even the same surname. Jasmine Turner. Friends for life, she thought.

"What was you two talkin' 'bout so earnestly?" Jasmine asked as the three girls linked arms and headed towards the main entrance of the intimidatingly large, ponderous old building that was their school. Its galaxy of windows were glinting as the sun broke through the clouds.

"Boys," said Donna promptly in reply to Jasmine.

"I ain't interested in boys," Jasmine said dismissively. "Not yet. I s'ppose it'll come, but I reckon all that stuff is more trouble than it's worth."

"You're in love with Jesus," Donna said provocatively.

"Sure, I am, but that's different," Jasmine protested. "Jesus is mah saviour. An' he'll be yours too if you let him." She had thickened her accent in a self-parody as she sometimes did in making these sorts of pronouncements.

"Donna's beyond saving!" Ruth laughed, feeling slightly guilty. They probably shouldn't tease Jasmine about how religious she was.

"*No*-one is beyond savin'! God's love is for everyone, all the time." Her face broke into her characteristic big smile. "Even Donna!"

"How about Stephen Orford?" Donna asked. "He's always getting into trouble. *And* he keeps on trying to make out with me!"

"You encourage him," Ruth pointed out.

"I can't help being irresistible! Anyway, I'm in training for when I become a homecoming queen!"

"You and your homecoming queen," Jasmine said in her normal voice. "Vanity, vanity, all is vanity!" She was laughing as she quoted the Bible.

"Just you see! They'll fall at my feet!"

They probably will, Ruth thought as, unlinking arms, the girls entered the middle-school building along with other pupils. Being a homecoming queen was not an ambition of hers at all – just as well, she supposed, as she would never get chosen anyway – but she couldn't stop, and didn't want to stop, and didn't try to stop, thoughts of Greg constantly occupying her mind.

During the rest of the school day, she was chided several times by teachers for not concentrating. Which was unfair because she *was* concentrating – just not on her schoolwork.

iv

When Ruth arrived home that afternoon, her dad was up a ladder, half-hidden behind the beginnings of a cascade of wisteria, secateurs in one hand, a trail of garden twine dangling from a pocket, as he concentrated on reattaching the climber where it had become detached from the trellis.

"Hi, Dad!" Ruth blew him a kiss and darted into the house and up to her bedroom to change. What should she wear? The pale-yellow dress again? Or the dark-red nautical dress, with the white collar and blue ribbons? She held them up in turn in front of David Cassidy, asking, "Which one? Which one?"

Car sounds. She looked out of the window, down into the parking area where tufts of grass were showing between the paving slabs. Her uncle's 'tank' had come to a halt by the garage and its doors were opening. She watched as uncle, aunt, Brad, and finally Greg emerged from it. Greg, not Brad, was wearing the bomber jacket, but the two of them were sharing some sort of joke, with Brad clowning about, Greg laughing at him.

A pang of jealousy. Turning, she threw the pale-yellow on to the bed from where it slid to the floor, hurriedly put on the red nautical, gave her hair a rapid brushing, and ran downstairs, nearly tripping on the way, to join them all in the sitting room. Her dad was already holding forth about wisteria.

"Hi," she said in general, hoping Greg would reply. He did give her a brief wave, but continued listening to her dad. Brad ignored her, Aunt Lou smiled effusively, and Mom motioned to indicate that something was wrong with Ruth's dress. One wing of her dress's collar was folded back. Ruth quickly adjusted it.

"Some species climb up clockwise," Dad concluded his explanation, rotating a finger in demonstration, "and others go counterclockwise." His finger reversed direction. "I don't know how they decide which way to go. It's all very, er," he paused and smiled round at his audience, "*wisteri-us.*"

Ruth had heard the joke before, as had the rest of the family, but Greg groaned politely, not, however, this time throwing his head back to laugh outright, saying instead, "You should meet one of the friends I mentioned yesterday, George. Phil. He's a pun-meister. You could give him a run for his money."

*

The evening meal over, Ruth's mom and aunt were tidying up and chatting in the kitchen; their husbands were outside, examining something to do with the guttering; and Brad, having talked with Greg through much of the meal about rock music, was slouched in a chair, thumbing through old copies of *Reader's Digest*, laughing occasionally; and Greg showed Ruth some of his sketchbook drawings.

A glorious quarter of an hour for her as he slowly turned the pages: sketches he had done on the airplane coming over, at the wedding reception, during his New York sightseeing, and in the Greyhound coach. But most of the pages were full of fragmentary images – she looked at a church door repeated several times from different angles, with scribbled notes about its location and colouring; then at tree bark seen from a distance, from close up, from very close up, again with notes added; at a dirty, broken bottle lying on its side; at a rather horrible sketch of a dead bird with tiny things crawling on it; at a page of elbows and hands and individual fingers pointing or curled up or somewhere in between.

"That's *so* neat," she said, sighing as he closed the sketchbook. "Thank you *so* much, Greg. It's wonderful."

"Thank you, Ruthie! Now, do I get to see some of your work?"

"Would you like to?"

"Yeah, certainly would."

"They're upstairs, in my room."

Greg held up a hand. "Let's have a look at them down here."

"Some of my best ones are on the walls. Well," suddenly worried she was boasting, "the ones I like best."

"All the same, better bring them down."

"Okay."

She dashed upstairs, and it was only as she charged into her room that she realized how *gross* it would have been if Greg had come up and seen the David Cassidy collage. A narrow escape from terminal embarrassment.

She darted about, collecting a selection of drawings and paintings from table and walls, then trembling slightly returned to the sitting room. Mom and Aunt Lou had reappeared from the kitchen and were sharing family news in low voices. Ruth resumed her place on the sofa next to Greg.

"Woo, quite a portfolio!" Greg picked up the top item, the cat on the tree branch, and studied it intently.

"This is great," he said after an agonizing minute that lasted half an hour.

"Is it all right?" *Please like it*, she was saying silently to herself. *Please. Please.*

"All right? It's more than all right," Greg said, still examining it closely. "It's exceptionally good. A touch of the Cheshire cat?

Alice in Wonderland? This is another cat with character, and you feel that, well, you could reach out and stroke its fur. Has it got a name?"

"I don't know his actual name, but I call him Smokey, because that's his colour. I'm not too sure about the branch he's on, though."

"Mmm, I was just wondering about that, too; maybe it's... poor old Smokey doesn't look entirely safe, maybe a little more shading here," he pointed, "and here...would give it more...make it more solid." He turned his head to look at her as she nodded and bit her bottom lip, no longer worried about letting him see the brace on her teeth. His hair had flopped forward, and he must have shaved recently but carelessly. She could see specks of what she supposed was dried blood on his neck and throat.

"Let's see some more." Greg put Smokey down and took up a study of wildflowers: primroses, primulas, and wood anemones. "Good detail. You have a terrific eye."

*

"The secret," Greg said, a dozen or more Ruth pictures later, each receiving praise, some more than others, "as I guess you know, is to draw, draw, draw! Keep on drawing! Never be without a sketch pad and pencils. Anything that catches your eye, do a quick sketch. Make notes. Anything. Doesn't have to be pretty-pretty; draw ordinary things, draw boring things, draw ugly things. But draw what you see, not what you think you ought to see. Yeah?"

"Yeah," said Ruth, using the word self-consciously. "Miss Abrams said something like that. You don't see a circle as a circle if you look at it from an angle, so don't draw it as a circle."

"That's it. She's your teacher? She's lucky to have a pupil with your ability. Or is your entire class made up of artistic geniuses?"

"Oh no!" Ruth flushed with pleasure. "Sorry if it sounds like boasting, but I probably am the best. Donna, she's my best friend, is terrible at art, but she's not bothered by it. Jasmine's not bad, but she's much better at singing and wants to become a singer when she's older. Or a pastor."

"Or a singing pastor? And what about – Dana?"

"Donna. She can't sing either! But she's ever so much fun. I've done several sketches of her if you want to see them as well?"

"Yeah, show me."

Ruth flipped through her sketchbook to find the one of Donna she considered her best.

"Hey, that's very good! What does she want to do when she's grown up? If she's not going to be an artist or a singer or a pastor!"

Ruth considered. What *did* Donna want? Difficult to tell. "She does want to be a homecoming queen one day," she offered.

"A what?"

"A homecoming queen. *You* know."

"I'm afraid I don't. Though I know it's in a Monkees' song." He started to sing 'Daydream Believer', and she suddenly remembered.

"Oh yes, Ted used to sing that. He's a lot older than me. Older than Brad. I thought that was the Beatles."

She heard Brad snort.

"Wash your mouth out!" Greg said in a teasing tone. "No comparison. The Beatles are the greatest ever. But yeah, the Monkees did some good stuff, and in that one there's a line about a homecoming queen. I've never known what it meant, though."

"Oh well, I can tell you!" Ruth exclaimed excitedly. "It's when, you know, people go off to college after high school, and when they come back home the first time, there's a big celebration to welcome them – like a party or a, you know, football game, and a girl is voted as being the homecoming queen and all the boys want to dance with her and, you know…" She lapsed into an embarrassed silence, suddenly uncertain whether she should be saying all that.

"Sounds a bit like being a May Queen, and she wants to be one? Well, if your drawing of her is anything like – and it really is good – I reckon she'd make a good one in time But it's not exactly a job for life! You don't want to be one?"

"Not really. I haven't got the face for it, have I?"

"Hey! Don't do yourself down. You have a much more *interesting* face."

The word interesting sounded to her as if it were the highest praise possible. She glowed.

"In fact," Greg continued, "I know what I'd like to do." Without explaining any further, he stood up, said, "I'll be back in a minute. If you want, feel free to look through this other one," and left the room, first pausing to ask her mom something, who smiled and nodded.

As Ruth picked up the second sketchbook, Aunt Lou asked, "Are you finding it helpful, poppet?"

"Oh yes! Really wonderful. He is *so* good!"

"Don't you go hogging all his attention," Mom put in.

"I won't, I won't! But he said I could look at this."

Mom and Aunt Lou resumed chatting in low voices. She turned the book pages slowly and reverently, as though they were made of glass and liable to shatter if she didn't exercise extreme caution, although the robust cartridge paper was a far better quality than the pads she used.

At one page of drawings, she started giggling. Greg, returning with a hard-backed dining-room chair, looked at what was making her laugh. She had turned to a page full of noses of all different sizes and shapes: bulbous and pointy and squashed and turned-up and bent and hooked and button and flaring and hairy and one or two (how disgusting) dripping; and seen from all different angles, full-on and side-on and from above and from below.

"You like them?" he asked.

"They're so funny! They're really neat."

"Yeah, noses can be funny," Greg agreed. "There's a famous story by a Russian writer called Gogol about a nose that left a man's face and went on to have a life of its own. It's very clever. Very funny."

"Goggle?"

"Gogol. G, O, G, O, L. It's probably a bit too old for you at the moment, but you could always try writing your own story about a nose."

"I'm not very good at writing. But Donna likes writing. That *is* something she's ever so good at. She could write it."

"And you could illustrate it! Now then, Ruthie," he had put the dining chair down several feet away from the settee where she was sitting, "I'm going to do some drawing, if I could have the pad back."

"What are you going to draw?"

"You." He sat down.

"Me?"

"You! Or to be more precise, your face. As I said, you have a very interesting face. Do you mind if I draw it?"

"No. No, of course not." She couldn't control her voice going shriller. "You want to draw my face?"

"Uh-huh." He was busy attaching the sketch pad, open at a fresh page, to a board using metal clips. "Then if you like," his voice distorted by a pencil clamped between his teeth, "I'll do just your nose to add to my collection! Right. Now, Ruthie," he removed the pencil, "turn your head away from me – no, not that far – turn back a bit – that's it. Now tilt your head back just a little – that's fine – the light's good like that. Try not to move, but it doesn't matter if you do. No, relax your face, don't put on a smile, just – that's it! I'll just…"

He did not complete the sentence. Ruth, in a happy daze, could hear the faint sound of his pencil moving about the pad.

V

School lunchbreak in bright spring weather. With Ruth in the middle, the three girls were strolling around in the school grounds, arms round each other's waists. Other pupils were clustered in twos and threes and larger groups, talking, laughing, giggling, arguing, shouting; some solitaries were sitting on walls, reading, staring into space, fiddling with their hair, their shoes. Nearby, several boys were shooting baskets, and from the tennis courts came the thwack! thwack! of games in progress, with intermittent cries of, "Let!", "Out!", "Mine!"

Ruth was catching her friends up on the previous evening.

"He did *what*?" Donna squealed.

"He drew my nose!"

"That's weird!"

"It's what artists do."

"What, go around drawing people's noses? Artists must be weird, then!" Donna said, adding in that know-it-all tone of voice she sometimes adopted, "Anyway, your nose is nothing to write home about."

"He thinks it is," Ruth pointed out. "Only he's not *writing*, is he? He's drawing."

"Well, if he wants to draw noses, he could draw mine! That way I'd get to meet him!"

"He should draw *mah* nose," Jasmine said in her extravagantly thick accent, flaring her nostrils and tilting her head back to show her nose in profile. "Or mah paw's!"

"They are something," Donna conceded.

"They're noble noses! That's what he say. Not like yo' tiddly whitey noses!"

All three of them laughed.

"I s'ppose you'll be around there again tonight, will you?" Donna asked, holding down her skirt as they turned a corner of the building into a breeze.

"No," Ruth said sadly. "My uncle and aunt have taken him somewhere."

"That's too bad."

"But guess what!" Ruth felt a rush of excitement as she remembered. "Tomorrow we're all going to Walden Pond! A whole day together!"

"Why're you going there? We've been there two or three times. It's all right," Donna shrugged, "but it's—"

"Nothing to write home about?" Ruth interrupted gleefully. "That's where you're wrong, Donna Smarty-pants! Greg wants to go there and see it because he says that man who lived by it in a log cabin was very important and we should be proud of him."

"Henry David Thoreau," Jasmine said in her normal accent. "My pa knows about him. He was telling me when we went there last fall. He's sort of one of Pa's heroes, 'cos although he was white he was an important abolitionist and went around giving talks about it, getting other people to agree with him."

"What's an abolis— what you said?" Donna asked.

"It's someone who was against slavery and wanted it abolished. They were known as abolitionists. They believed that

God loves everyone equally, an' nobody should be a slave. It's against the Bible."

"Greg knows a lot about him as well," Ruth said. "He was talking with Uncle last night before I had to go to bed, but I don't think Uncle approves of him. He said he wanted people to break the law which he shouldn't have, but Greg said he wanted to make sure the government didn't make laws that were unfair, like having slaves."

"He should have come to this school then!" Donna said. "There's a lot I'd like to see abolished."

"You ain't a slave," Jasmine said severely. As Donna looked embarrassed and Ruth choked off a laugh, Jasmine continued, "My ma's great-grandma was a slave."

"Really?" Ruth said. "I didn't know. How did that happen?"

"She jus' was when she was born," and as Jasmine told them more about her family history, Ruth wished she had understood more of what Greg and her uncle had been politely arguing about. Greg had sounded very knowledgeable, and she had realized that Uncle Harold had found it difficult to be contradicted, taking off his glasses and waving them about a lot.

Greg. It seemed that her thoughts were full of Greg all the time, only it wasn't thinking in the way that she had to think about how to solve a problem in arithmetic, or work out how to draw a complicated picture, or learn from Mom how to bake a cake. Thinking about Greg was more in the form of spontaneous scenes playing themselves out before her mind's eye and in her mind's ear. Scenes both of actual times with Greg, which then extended and developed themselves in ways that hadn't really occurred, and fanciful scenes with no basis in anything that had happened but she supposed could have: Greg kissing her cheek and the prickly unshaven feel of his cheeks, Greg sitting next to her on the settee; Greg smiling his lopsided smile at her; Greg (who knows?) enfolding her within the confines of his bomber jacket…

She was finding it almost physically painful to be parted from him, as though her stomach was being tugged out of her body. She craved reassurance that he liked her, that he thought she was clever, interesting, pretty, cute. Does he like her? Surely he does, but she so much wants him to say so, she wants him to say he likes her more than he likes anyone else. Donna's throwaway comment about letting Greg draw *her* nose had sent a major fluttery feeling through Ruth's entire body. She did *not* want Greg to meet Donna, because Donna is *lovely* and *pretty* and *cute*, and unwanted scenes in which Greg prefers Donna over her also keep playing on the film screen in her head.

"Hey," a boy's voice broke through. "Donna! You're looking neat today!"

"Get lost, Stephen!" Donna called back at a stocky boy sporting a severe crew cut and, contrary to school rules, blatantly chewing gum; but seeing the way her friend smiled, Ruth doubted she meant it.

Did Greg think she, Ruth, looked *neat*? No, not neat, British people didn't say neat, did they, like they didn't say sidewalk. What did they say, though, instead of neat? What did Greg say to girls he liked?

vi

"We're going to Concord first," Uncle Harold announced when Ruth and her parents arrived at the Watsons' mansion the next morning, "so we can show Greg the Minute Man and the shot that was heard round the world." Uncle Harold was wearing a pair of surfing trunks – all turquoise sea and a sky of garish reds and yellows. On his black tee shirt was the image of a gold-coloured extractor fan and the words *Keeping Cool with AirConPro*.

"What shot?" said Greg.

"It's about the war," Ruth said importantly.

"The War of Independence," Brad butted in. "The first shot was fired at Lexington, then there was the battle of Concord. There's a poem about it."

"And the Minute Man? Who he?"

"They were the local farmers and labourers," Uncle Harold said. "As soon as the British army was sighted, they'd drop whatever they were doing and be ready as an army within, er, well…"

"Within a mi*nute*," Ruth's Dad said, stressing the second syllable, as though the men in question were tiny. Today's m'Gandhi was a broad-brimmed sunhat, otherwise no concessions to leisure activity.

"Within a *min*ute," Uncle Harold pronounced it correctly.

"A sort of Dad's Army?" By the puzzled silence that followed, Ruth realized she wasn't alone in not understanding what Greg meant.

"*We're* all ready now." Aunt Lou, in slacks and a sensible top, broke the silence. "We should get going."

"Your shirt, honey." Ruth's mom pointed at her daughter. "Do it properly. I said not to tie it above your waist like that."

Ruth had seen in *Tiger Beat* ways to wear a cheesecloth shirt. Reluctantly she untied the loose knot, then hitched up her shorts, which were faded blue and longer than she liked.

Everyone else started moving, but she stayed near Uncle Harold's large black car, the tank, hoping she would be invited to ride in it with Greg and, annoyingly but unavoidably, Brad.

"Come on, Ruth." Mom, overdressed in a green outfit more suitable for church than a day's outing in spring, took her hand and steered her to their car.

There was some consolation in the way Greg said, "See you there, Ruthie – yeah?" to which, blushing, she replied with forced casualness, "Yeah!" and gave a little wave.

He returned the wave. "Got your sketch pad and stuff?"

"Yeah!"

"In you get, Ruth," Mom said firmly.

In she got.

"I do wish you wouldn't copy him like that," Mom grumbled as the cars moved off.

"Like what?"

"Saying *yeah* all the time. Will you please stop saying it."

Ruth bit her lip. If she were Donna, she would respond to this instruction with a cheeky, "Yeah!" but she couldn't bring herself to be quite that saucy. She mouthed "Yeah!" silently while imagining Greg smiling in approval at her cheek. She wriggled in pleasure.

*

Ruth had already seen the memorial to the shot heard round the world, a great grey obelisk built from granite blocks, and didn't think much of it. Greg, though, appeared to be fascinated, slowly circling it, taking photographs and making quick lines in his sketchbook.

"A touch of Cleopatra's Needle," he said on returning to the others, again, Ruth realized, puzzling everyone, "but not as tall or as old. But still impressive."

At the statue of the Minute Man on his stone plinth, alert and ready with his musket, Greg took more photographs, made more quick sketches.

"Some of our history," Uncle Harold said proudly. His balding head was shiny with sweat. "We might not have as much as you English, but what we have we're proud of!"

"Quality, not quantity." Ruth's dad nodded his agreement.

"It's an impressive casting," said Greg. "Bronze. There's a touch of the Apollo Belvedere about it. Not a criticism; quite the opposite."

"I was thinking more of what it celebrates," Uncle Harold insisted. "Wouldn't you say, George? Throwing off the English yoke?"

"Like Mahatma Gandhi!" Dad tapped his sunhat.

"No offence intended," said Uncle Harold.

"None taken." Greg gave his lopsided smile.

"Greg," Ruth asked tentatively, "do you ever do sculptures?"

"I've never tried it, Ruthie. I appreciate them, yeah, but doing it doesn't appeal. Outside my range. I feel you're too much

44

at the mercy of the material for my liking. Is it something you'd like to do?"

"Not really. I did some modelling in clay at summer camp last year, but it didn't really come out right."

"You made a nice pot," Aunt Lou said.

Ruth pulled a face. "It was all wonky."

"Well, we can't all be Michelangelo," Greg said. "Able to do everything. Concentrate on what you're good at."

They returned to the cars and resumed their journey, but after a few minutes the brake lights on Uncle Harold's car lit up as it pulled off the road.

"Now what?" Mom said as they also came to a halt. Everyone got out of the cars.

Two or three hundred yards away on the opposite side of the road stood a church, a long, gleaming white structure with a tall, sharp steeple. Ruth thought it somehow looked all wrong.

"Very odd," Greg voiced her thoughts. "The proportions don't work, do they? And I hope they've got an efficient lightning conductor! But that," he swung round and pointed to another building on their side of the road, also two or three hundred yards away, "that is quite something! I just had to have a decent look. Very John Constable, don't you think?"

For the third time that morning it was evident to Ruth that the others did not get his meaning. She did though, as only a few weeks ago the picture on Miss Abrams' apron had been *The Hay Wain*, and she had subsequently shown Ruth a book containing some of the English painter's best-known works. Ruth could see exactly what Greg meant. The building was a mill, its great waterwheel, almost as high as the greyish stone building itself, stationary, with an adjoining stone structure partially fallen in so that water was gushing from it. A dense bank of trees stood guard behind the building, with three more trees to one side, one of them half-toppled over and caught by the nearest of the other two; and a placid horse with what looked like a shaggy mane standing near the three trees, head half-turned in their direction, completed the scene. Sunlight from a clear sky glittered on the water and brought a warm glow to the stonework. Ruth, excitement mounting, told herself *very John Constable*.

"Won't be a moment, folks, but I must just…" Greg did not finish his sentence as he darted off, sketchbook already open.

Ruth also darted forward. She *had* to join him. But Mom caught her by the arm. "Oh no you don't, young lady!"

"Oh, please!"

"No, no," Dad said. "Let him be. He doesn't want little girls chasing him all the time."

Ruth winced. "I'm not a little girl."

"No, sweetheart, you're not a *little*, little girl."

"But you said—"

"I know, sweetheart. I didn't mean it unkindly. I only meant that you're rather younger than him." He put his arms round her. "I apologize! Forgive me?"

"All right!" She always enjoyed a Dad-cuddle. "I forgive you. Just this once!"

"My sins are forgiven. Let's all celebrate with some coffee while we're waiting for Greg. Where are the flasks?"

vii

She was still smarting from her Dad's remark, even though he had apologized, as they turned into the carpark at Walden Pond – why wasn't it called a lake? she wondered as she had done on a previous visit. The famous expanse of water could still be glimpsed through the woodland of maples and oaks and hickories, which were yet to come into full leaf.

They drove slowly past rows of parked cars, the sun flashing from front and rear windshields like a stroboscope, as they looked for somewhere to park, until Uncle Harold's tank turned abruptly to claim a space. A few cars further on Dad swung theirs into another space. Getting out, Ruth squinted, and scrabbled in her bag for sunglasses.

The cars' trunks were opened. Dad and Uncle Harold took out big bags of food and drinks. Aunt Lou handed Brad two folding chairs.

"You take the picnic basket, honey," Ruth's mom told her.

"Hey, that looks heavy. I'll take it," Greg said. "Ruthie, you carry my bag?"

"Yeah! I mean, sure!" *See! He does like me!*

As they set off, and with her own satchel of sketching material on her back, she carried Greg's bag with the same care as Pastor Gravatt handling the Bible. No swinging it back and forth at her side, no jerking it up and down or twisting it to and fro as she would normally do to entertain herself, but maintaining an even pace and keeping the bag as much as she could at the same height above the ground.

It was cool in the woodland, with sunlight flickering through the canopy. The range of greens already on show quickened Ruth's heart; she wished she could paint them all. Her previous visit had been during the fall, when the red oak and red maple had been ablaze, and she thought the picture she'd done of them, using the oil sticks, was one of her best. Buttercups now decorated the more open patches, and the path itself was crunchy underfoot with twigs and the detritus of hickory husks. The scent of the hickory mingled with those of pine and other trees; she tried to figure out what colours they would be if scents did have colour.

They stopped at a little cove and gazed across the pond, where a breeze was creating ripples. A skein of geese flew across, honking loudly.

"There's a heron," Brad said, pointing at a distant figure that could have been carved from stone.

"Good eyesight," Greg said.

"You can sometimes see kingfishers here," Dad said. They all stood still and gazed about them with varying degrees of intensity, but were out of luck.

They moved on. Greg loped, Ruth thought, rather than walked; free and easy, rather like a lion or a leopard, taking only two paces to every three of Dad's and Uncle Harold's, which made her smile. It reminded her of the old-fashioned comedy films Dad watched when they came on the television.

"You got anything like this to compare in England?" Uncle Harold asked Greg as though he assumed the answer had to be no.

"Every place is unique," Greg raised a hand like Pastor Gravatt in the pulpit, "but yeah, there are great places near where I live. I was brought up on Dartmoor—"

"That's where *The Hound of the Baskervilles* is, isn't it?" Brad interrupted.

"You're right. The Great Grimpen Mire and all that. You like Sherlock Holmes?"

"I sure do!" Brad started to list the stories he knew. Soon he and Greg were debating the merits of individual adventures, and Ruth felt out of it. She had only vaguely heard of the detective.

A discussion started among the others about where and when to have their picnic, concluding when Aunt Lou said firmly, "Let's first show Greg where Thoreau's cabin was, and then find one of the picnic areas."

*

As Ruth already knew from her previous visit, the cabin no longer existed; instead, a rough circle of rectangular blocks of granite, each about three feet high, marked the place, and by a cairn of rough stones there was a wooden plaque inscribed with a quotation. Greg went down on his haunches in front of it. Ruth stood beside him, with everyone else clustered behind them like a backing group. Uncle Harold was fiddling with his camera.

" 'I went to the woods because I wished to live deliberately,' " Greg read out, " 'to front only the essential facts of life' – odd way of putting it – 'and see if I could not learn what it had to teach, and not, when I came to die, discover that I had not lived.' Wow, that's saying something."

"What does it mean?" Ruth said, hoping it was a sensible thing to ask.

"Good question." Greg stood up. "He's basically saying that you should live so that when you're about to kick the bucket you don't regret what you've done or not done with your life. Which I wouldn't argue with."

"He means die," Dad said cheerfully, "bite the big one."

"Join the choir invisible," Greg added. "Bereft of life."

"Sounds morbid to me," Mom grumbled.

"He didn't exactly contribute to society, did he?" Uncle Harold insisted.

"Oh, I don't know so much, Harold." Greg gave his lopsided smile. "Helping raise people's awareness of the evils of slavery strikes me as pretty significant. Yeah?"

Yeah, Ruth thought, remembering Jasmine talking about her family's background in slavery.

"I believe," Dad's tone of voice told Ruth another of his not very funny comments was on its way, "that he acted more in Thoreau than in anger."

"Oh, very good." Greg made a hand-clapping gesture. "Punmeister Phil would be proud of you."

At that, Ruth laughed to show she had got Dad's joke.

"Picnic time," Aunt Lou announced firmly. "There's that place we used last time a bit further along."

They moved on. Brad picked up a stick and started swishing it about. One random swish struck Greg's arm.

"Careful, Brad," his father warned, but Greg picked up another stick and began a sword fight with Brad.

"Have at you, sirrah!" he cried, and Brad, laughing, fell to the ground. "So dies another foe of good King George!" Greg proclaimed.

"He wasn't good!" Brad protested from the ground as Greg placed a foot on his chest. "He oppressed us! Down with tyrants!"

"That, sirrah, is treason!" Greg stepped back, held out a hand, and pulled Brad back to his feet.

Afraid that Greg would continue fooling about with Brad, Ruth quickly asked him, "Would you like to live here?"

Greg turned to her. "I like the idea in theory!"

"Me too!"

"But I'm not sure about it in practice," Greg added. "Too much like hard work, chopping wood and digging potatoes."

Walking next to Greg, she listened as a conversation developed between him and Dad and Uncle Harold about England and its government. He did not support the Conservatives and disapproved of the British prime minister.

"Their trouble is with the unions," Dad said.

"What are they?" she asked.

"The workers," said her uncle. "They're getting above themselves, trying to bring the government down. Good old Ted Heath's having none of it though. He's going to put them in their place."

Greg asked something about the American president. He didn't refer to him as good old Richard Nixon but as Tricky Dicky. The conversation ended as they arrived at a picnic area with a view over the water.

*

Lunch over, more walking was proposed. Mom and Aunt Lou both said no, they would sit and enjoy the view while letting their food go down, an expression Ruth always found rather disgusting.

"Coming, Greg?" her dad asked.

"Thanks, but," Greg held up his bag, "I wouldn't mind staying hereabouts for a while to do a spot of sketching. I want to take some New England wildlife back to Ye Merrie Olde England!"

"Ruth?"

"I'll stay and do some sketching as well," she said quickly, holding up her own bag.

"If that's okay with Greg?" Dad looked enquiringly at him.

"I think you should go for a walk with the others," Mom said. "Let Greg do what he does undisturbed."

"That's okay." Greg was rummaging in his bag. "You won't disturb me, Ruthie. It's good to have a little colony of artists!" He looked up at her and smiled. "We'll be the Devon and Massachusetts Artists Collective. Commissions by appointment. Brad, will you join us?" He held up a small sketching pad. "You could borrow this."

Ruth felt a pang of horror. Not Brad. Just her and Greg, please. *Please.*

To her relief, Brad shook his head. "I'll walk. I'm no good at drawing and stuff."

"Very well, sirrah!" Greg proclaimed. "We'll see you anon!"

After a brief discussion between Aunt Lou and Dad about when they would all regather, the walkers set off. Mom and Aunt Lou settled themselves on the folding chairs to enjoy the scenery and 'let their food go down'. This usually entailed falling asleep. Which is what they promptly did. Greg, who had been wandering around in the vicinity, returned. "There's a good place up there where we can both sit," he told Ruth, "if that's okay? Or would you prefer to be on your own?"

"I'd like to be with you." Ruth could feel her face grow hot and hoped her blushes weren't too conspicuous.

"Okay, that's fine."

Her heart seemed to be thumping hard as they went and settled themselves, Greg on a flat rock covered with moss and lichen, Ruth on a tree stump with four large flat fungi like a series of steps growing out of its side.

She organized her bits and pieces and wondered what to sketch. Already Greg's absorption in his work looked absolute, and she chided herself for not concentrating properly. But how could she with Greg so close by, with his pale blue eyes, his floppy hair, his stubbly cheeks and chin? Why not, though, combine looking at Greg and sketching? Soon she too was absorbed.

*

Greg came across to Ruth and stood behind her. Too late she turned the page to hide her efforts. He reached over her shoulder and gently turned the page back.

"That's me!" he exclaimed.

Ruth bit her lip and nodded.

"I'm flattered! Hey, Ruthie, that's really good, even though it is my old mug. I like the look you've put in my eyes!" he continued. "It makes me look...um...deep and meaningful!"

"Well, you are clever," she ventured.

"That's not a universally acknowledged truth."

"Would you mind signing it?"

"It's usually the artist who signs it!"

"Please."

"Okay. Let's both sign it."

Ruth signed the portrait of Greg, and he signed 'Gregory Adams' at the top of the picture as though it were the title. Beneath his name he added '(a true and telling likeness)'.

"Thank you! That's so neat!" Ruth felt herself glowing with pride.

"Now it's my turn to draw you."

"Oh no," she said, horror replacing the glow. "You don't want to do that. Not again."

"Yes. Again! And not just your face this time. Full length."

He squatted directly in front of her, and she found herself looking directly into his eyes. As he maintained a steady gaze, the surroundings of trees and undergrowth and the sunlight on the water seemed to disappear and all she remained conscious of was looking into Greg's eyes and him looking into hers. He was neither smiling nor frowning but completely relaxed, and as she too relaxed there came a sensation of floating, of warmth, of stillness, of peace.

"I'd like to capture that look of yours," Greg eventually said in a quiet voice. "Don't move."

Right then she couldn't have moved even had she wanted to as Greg, retrieving his pad, made a few quick marks on it, paused, then made a few more.

"Wonderful," he said, as though to himself, while continuing to sketch. As well as blinking as little as possible, she tried at first to make her breathing imperceptible.

"You are allowed to breathe, you know," Greg said after a while.

Ruth relaxed.

"That's fine."

She had no idea how much time had passed when the sound of her dad calling them broke in. "Would Rembrandt and Michelangelo care to join us?"

"With you soon!" Greg called back, and a couple of minutes later he was done, standing up and stretching.

"You make a great model," he told her.

"Can I see?" she asked hesitantly.

"Sure." He held it up to her. "Don't forget, it's not the same as looking in a mirror. Left becomes right and right becomes left."

"Gee," was all she could say. It was, somehow, unbelievably perfect. Looking at it, she could begin to believe that she too might be *pretty* and *cute*. Wait until she told Donna on Monday!

But as she rejoined the others, she had to work hard to avoid thinking about the looming disaster of tomorrow.

viii

Sunday, the day after the Walden Pond trip, Ruth already knew would be the last full day of Greg's visit. His Greyhound would be leaving first thing Monday morning, taking him back to New York for a day's sightseeing before he caught the flight back to England. She had, however, managed until then, if not to forget this, at least to disregard it, blinded by the light of the approaching Walden Pond expedition. But now that outing was in the past, its dazzling promise behind her, she woke on the Sunday morning with the full horror striking her, making her jerk upright in bed: *this is my last day with Greg!*

In church that morning when Pastor Gravatt told everyone to close their eyes and bow their heads in prayer, while he reminded God that He was almighty and gracious and that they were all sinners, she had prayed her own fervent prayer: *Please God, let Greg stay. Please let him stay. I pray that you will have mercy on me and grant my prayer...* only stopping when her mom nudged her as the congregation stood up to sing a hymn. But even as everyone else launched into 'Holy, Holy, Holy! Lord God Almighty', her silent prayer resumed.

That afternoon, they drove over to the mansion. As they got out of the car Ruth could hear shouts of "Here, to me!" and "Come on, Tom, over here!" and "Kick the thing!" Greg, Brad and three or four other boys were round the side of the house kicking a soccer ball about. Ruth went and watched as the shouting continued, willing Greg to turn and see her.

"Come on, honey." Her mom came up and took her by the arm.

"I'll just watch a bit."

"Don't get cold. It's turned chilly."

"I'm okay, Mom."

"Let's go in, Nancy," Dad called.

"Coming, George, coming. Don't be long, Ruth."

Ruth heard but did not reply. Greg had kicked the ball to Brad, who in turn kicked it to one of the others, the one called Tom, a gangly, dark-haired boy Ruth didn't know but had seen Brad with before. Tom missed the ball, and scampered after it as it came directly towards her. He scooped it up a few feet from her, then stood there, catching his breath.

"Hi," he panted. "You're Ruth, aren't you?" He sounded shy.

"Yes." She did not want Tom to talk to her. She wanted Greg to.

"You gonna to join us?"

She shook her head. When she was a year or two younger, before Ted had started college, she had had some fun times kicking the ball about with her two cousins, but that had changed. Ted was rarely there, and Brad had grown grumpy.

At last! Greg had seen her and was waving. She jumped up and down, frantically waving in return. Surely he would come to talk to her now? But he didn't. Tom had turned and kicked the ball back, and Greg stopped waving to go loping after it.

Disappointed, Ruth trudged indoors. In the main room Mom and Dad were settling down to play bridge with her uncle and aunt. She went into one of the other rooms, one that Uncle Harold called his snug. It smelled of old tobacco smoke:

the remnants of two thin cigars occupied a brass ashtray on a small round table near the main window. The table was flanked by a pair of imposing dark leather armchairs, angled so their occupants could gaze through the window onto the large expanse of grass where the soccer was currently being played. Several of Uncle Harold's precision diagrams, framed in wood, adorned the walls of the snug.

For several minutes Ruth slumped in one of the chairs, watching miserably as Greg continued to play with Brad and the other boys. Then suddenly she jumped to her feet and grabbed her sketching bag: if she couldn't be with Greg, if she couldn't talk to him, she could at least draw him. Draw him running, draw him kicking the ball, draw him doing what he was doing now – cleverly flicking the ball from foot to knee and up to his head, then letting it drop to his foot again.

Outside, she moved a folding green canvas chair to where she could sit without the sun in her eyes. Comfortable enough. Turning to a fresh sheet in the sketching pad, and taking up a pencil, she set to work.

Before long, frustrated and cross, she abandoned the attempt. Hopeless. She still didn't have any real idea how to go about drawing something that was moving. How were you meant to draw something when everything about it was different from second to second? Miss Abrams had made a suggestion about it recently when she had been trying to draw Donna and Jasmine dancing, but it hadn't helped. She would ask Greg about it. He could show her. But could he? Would he? And when? He'd be off in the morning while she was at school, then when he was back in England, would he write her? Surely he would write her. She'd definitely write him straightaway, even while he was on the plane – his address! Panic surged up. She didn't know his address – but immediately the panic subsided – Mom would have it, and so would Aunt Lou.

But writing him was all very well – when would she *see* him again? Would he come over for another visit? Could she go over there? To England? How old would she have to be before her parents let her travel alone?

She falls into a reverie in which she sees an adult, sophisticated Ruth Whitehead, seasoned transatlantic traveller, descending from a plane at whatever the airport at London is called, raising a hand in greeting to her darling distant relative who would now be close again, who eagerly waves at her from behind the barrier, then enfolds her in his arms and holds her tightly. She looks up into those lovely blue eyes as he gazes down at her, and then—

"Hello, Ruthie! You look miles away!" Greg's voice broke in. He looked dishevelled, slightly muddy, and he was breathing heavily. "What have you been up to? Sketching? Excellent. What of?"

"Oh, you know," she said vaguely. "All of you doing the soccer. It's difficult isn't it, trying to draw people who're moving? Or anything that's moving."

"That's the big advantage of doing still life! Or people posing for you. Anyway, I must have a shower, or no-one'll want to be near me! See you."

"See you."

Greg didn't return, even after enough time for him to have had several showers. What was he doing? Sleeping? Writing letters? Or, horror of horrors, simply avoiding her? No, no, surely not – but panic again welled up and this time did not subside. Agitated, she sprang to her feet.

"You gonna play, Ruth?" Tom called. The boys had continued playing without Greg.

"Come on, Ruth," Brad also called cajolingly. Ruth shook her head, grabbed her bag, and ran back into the house. There was no sign of Greg. She could hear Dad and Uncle talking in the main sitting room, and Mom and Aunt in the kitchen. She retreated to the snug again and wallowed in misery before being called to help set the table for the evening meal.

*

Task done, Ruth slipped away to the bathroom. At least Greg would be with them all for the rest of the evening and she had come prepared. As well as her sketching bag she had brought another bag, containing her best dress, her best hairband, and the pair of party shoes she really liked. She had also, guiltily but, she thought, bravely, 'borrowed' and brought with her the remnants of a lipstick from Mom's dressing table drawer.

She locked the door to the large bathroom with its pale pink fittings, fluffy white towels, and most important of all, a large wall-mounted mirror. Like much of the house, it spoke far more of Aunt Lou than Uncle Harold.

Off with her boring dress, on with its replacement – lime green, sleeveless, with small buttons all the way down from its high neck to her waist. Bought when Aunt Lou had taken her shopping in the new year. Shoes on, then a careful brushing of her hair and on with the matching hairband.

That done, she took up the lipstick and, peering into the mirror, started to apply it as carefully as possible, in the way she had occasionally seen Mom doing. More recently, amidst much giggling in the girls' school bathroom, Donna had given her and Jasmine a brief initiation into the mysteries of make-up.

It didn't look quite right. Tearing off some bathroom tissue, she dabbed at her lips, applied a little more lipstick, and dabbed again. The red had strayed outside the border of her lips, looking like the time Dad had painted the skirting board in the sitting room. She wiped off the excess. Better, although the lighting wasn't all that helpful.

Someone tried the door.

"Sorry," she called out as a little spurt of panic hit her. "Just coming."

Pushing her discarded clothes, hairbrush and the lipstick into her bag, she unlocked the door and stepped out to find Aunt Lou waiting.

"Sorry," she repeated breathlessly.

"That's all right, poppet." Then, "My! You're looking good!"

Ruth moved to one side, but instead of going into the bathroom, Aunt Lou bent down and studied Ruth's face. "Oh, my! I think you've overdone it a little."

"Isn't it all right?"

"Go into my bedroom. I'll join you when I've finished in here."

The bedroom colours were also pink and white, and Ruth wondered if her aunt particularly liked marshmallows and candyfloss. She sat at the dressing table with its array of Aunt Lou's pots and jars and atomizers and little jewel boxes, hairbrushes of different sizes, and a large tortoiseshell comb. She was admiring an ornate hand mirror when Aunt Lou bustled in and closed the door.

"That's it, you stay on the chair, Ruth. Now, have you worn lipstick before?"

Ruth shook her head.

"Hmm. I thought not. Does my sister know you've got it? It's hers, I'm guessing."

Ruth nodded.

"Well, let's just get it looking right, shall we? Then I'll have a word with Nancy. If she says anything, I'm on your side. All right? It's Greg, isn't it?"

"Is it obvious?"

"Only to those who've got eyes to see. If it's any help, I had a mad crush on a much older boy when I was, well, maybe a year or so older than you are. Your mother was very sarcastic at the time – but that's older sisters for you. Mind you, she had her moments too. Right, hold still."

She spat on a handkerchief. Ruth flinched.

"Hmm, maybe not!" She took another handkerchief from the dressing table drawer, dampened it in a glass of water on the bedside table, and gently dabbed at Ruth's lips.

"Now then, hold *really* still. I'll do your lower lip first. No, don't purse them. That's it."

It was like having to sit still to have your portrait done, she thought, but not taking anything like as long. Aunt Lou worked quickly, applying a fresh tracing of lipstick, dabbing Ruth's lips with a dry piece of the handkerchief, then saying, "Take a look in the mirror."

Ruth took a look. "Oh, wow! That's so good!"

"It suits you, I must say. Provided you don't overdo it."

"It's fab! Thank you so much, Aunt Lou!"

"At your age it's best to be discreet, so no-one can quite tell if you're wearing make-up or not. Now," she picked up a little pot containing something pinkish, and a tiny brush with a thick cluster of soft bristles, "an itsy-bitsy touch of my rouge – I think your cheeks need it. Mind you," she added roguishly, "they'll redden up when you blush anyway! That's it… Now, head up! Be cheerful and charming!"

Ruth leapt up. "Thank you, thank you, thank you!"

"Off you go! No, don't kiss me! We don't want to smudge the lipstick, do we!"

Cheerful and charming, Ruth repeated to herself as she left the bedroom. She would be *cheerful and charming* for Greg.

Here goes, she thought a minute later as, heart thumping, she entered the sitting room where everyone else was now gathered. *Cheerful and charming.*

ix

"Well, well! What a vision!" her mom exclaimed. "I do believe this is in your honour, Greg! Well done, honey."

"Ruth!" her uncle called out, and as she turned round his camera flashed.

"Will you take one of me and Greg?" she asked in a rush before she could stop herself.

"Yeah, good idea!" Greg said. "The Massachusetts and Devon Artists Collective!" and there he was by her side, putting an arm round her shoulders.

The camera flashed again.

"And another." Greg knelt down, so he became almost her height. This time he put his arm round her waist; emboldened, she put her arm round his shoulders. The camera flashed for a third time, then a few more times.

"Okay, let's get a group photograph," Uncle Harold decided. He was attaching his camera to a tripod. "Nancy, you go there next to George..." He directed each where to stand, putting Ruth next to Brad at the front, and making sure of a space where he would stand once he had set the timer and pressed the shutter release. "Here we go," he said after several squints through the viewfinder. "Five seconds. Everyone smile." He hurried to his place.

He had put Greg immediately between but behind Ruth and Brad. As she froze in readiness for the flash, Ruth felt a hand resting on her right shoulder; from the corner of her right eye, she could see Greg's other hand on Brad's left shoulder.

The camera mechanism whirred; there came the flash and the click of the shutter.

"One more." Uncle Harold returned to the camera. "Stay where you are, everyone."

Photography done, they moved into the dining room. Both Ruth and Brad waited until Greg had sat down, then Brad, nearest to him, immediately claimed the seat on his right. Aunt Lou was about to take the seat on his left, but then, smiling at Ruth, offered it to her.

"Thanks," Ruth mouthed.

A little later Uncle Harold did the rounds, a bottle of wine in each hand, asking everyone, "Sweet or dry?"

"Can I have some, please?" she asked as her uncle passed her by.

"You're not old enough yet," Mom said.

"Brad's got some."

"He's older than you, honey."

"Just a taste. Please."

She heard Dad singing softly in his tuneless way something about honey tasting sweeter than wine, then, "Go on, then," he added, "I think she should, Nancy. Special occasion."

"Yes, I suppose so." Mom patted her hair. "They do grow up quickly, don't they?"

"They sure do," said Aunt Lou. "We certainly did!"

Uncle Harold poured a small amount of wine into a glass and placed it in front of her. "This is the sweet one; probably more to your taste."

She looked at Greg. "What are you having?"

"I like a spot of dry," Greg said.

"Can't I have dry as well?" to her mom.

"Women usually prefer sweet," her aunt said. "Give it a try."

She gave it a try. What was so special about it? It was all right, she supposed. The meal got under way and she gave the wine another try. Was it her imagination, or did it somehow go up to her head more than it went down to her stomach? With the third try she decided that she definitely liked it. It was making her want to giggle, but that wouldn't be *grown-up*, would it? No-one else was giggling.

A little later, as her uncle made the rounds again with the wine, she asked if she could try the other one, wondering why it was called dry when it was obviously just as wet as the sweet wine.

"I think you've had enough, honey," Mom said.

"Just a sip?" Pleadingly. "So that I know?"

"She could..." Not finishing his sentence, Greg held up an interrogative glass instead.

"Go on, then," Mom conceded.

Ruth drank a little from Greg's glass, making sure her lips went exactly where she could see his lips had been. A second, longer sip followed. No, Aunt Lou had been right, she preferred the sweet, but this was quite nice all the same. The earlier desire to giggle had faded, and now she felt an intense happiness as well as – what? A little giddiness, as though she'd been too long on a playground merry-go-round. She supposed this meant she was getting a little...*tiddly*, that's the word she'd heard Mom use sometimes. Tiddly.

After the meal, they all sat round in the main room to play paper and pencil games. As the youngest, Ruth got to pick a letter at random by closing her eyes and taking a tile out of the Scrabble bag. It was a C. Brad, as second youngest, chose the topic. Sports players. They had two minutes – Uncle Harold timed it – to write down the names of as many sports players whose names began with C as they could think of. Then everyone in turn read out their list. One point for every name, and two points for names no-one else had put down.

Brad won.

In the second game, Brad picked an M, and when Ruth chose the topic of artists everyone other than Greg groaned. Another two minutes, followed by the reading out of lists. When Ruth won – just beating Greg – she was too happy to be suspicious. The merry-go-round sensation had faded to a mild headache.

They divided up. Her dad and uncle hunched over the backgammon board, providing an intermittent background rattle of dice; Mom and Aunt Lou sat and gossiped; Ruth played rummy with Brad and Greg. She won once, Brad won once, and Greg won four times. For more than a blissful hour Ruth was able to disregard the onrushing future.

The dam broke as the evening was ending. They were all standing around in the capacious hallway, saying their goodbyes, discussing times, routes and future plans, as well as giving Greg numerous messages "for the English branch of our great family" as Uncle Harold put it. Ruth, on the edge of the group, tried to push between Dad and Aunt Lou, but Brad was blocking her way. Was he doing it deliberately? She became increasingly agitated. The happiness of the evening, of all the past few days, had now given way to desperate anguish. She was not being allowed to say goodbye properly to Greg. Didn't *anyone* realize or understand how she felt? Even Aunt Lou seemed to have forgotten.

She reached out and shoved Brad's shoulder. As he half turned towards her, a slight gap opened. She was immediately through and flung herself on Greg, clutching him round the waist, crying out, "Please don't go! Please, please, please, please,

please. Please stay. Don't go." And she buried her face in his clothes, sobbing.

"Now come on, honey…" she dimly heard her mom say.

"Hey, it's okay, yeah…"

"Ruth, now don't embarrass the poor man," was her dad's contribution. "England's wet enough as it is."

"No embarrassment!"

She felt herself being pulled back by someone, and her grip on Greg loosened.

"Leave her, Brad," Aunt Lou said. "Don't interfere. Let her be."

"But she's being—"

"Quiet!"

I must look a mess, Ruth thought despairingly as Greg, further loosening her grip, knelt down in front of her. Taking hold of her hands, he looked straight in her face.

"Hey, Ruthie," he said gently, "I do need to go. England expects, and all that. But it's been lovely meeting you. Best bit of my trip!"

"You will come again?" she asked chokingly.

"Yeah, sure I will!"

"Will you write me? Send me a card?"

"Yeah, sure I will. Will you write to me?"

She nodded.

"Promise?"

She nodded again. "I'll tell you what I've been drawing and painting."

"Great. Any chance you'll be able to send me copies sometimes?"

"I'd like to," she said doubtfully.

"I can see to that," Uncle Harold offered. There was a catch in his voice. "We've got a fancy new Xerox at the works. State of the art."

She felt Greg kiss her forehead, and then he slowly stood up. She desperately hoped he wasn't smiling or grinning at the others.

"We'd better be on our way," Mom said. "Come on, honey. Thanks, Lou. Thank you, Harold. It's been lovely."

"Where's m'Gandhi got to?" Dad was saying.

Aunt Lou helped Ruth to her feet and cuddled her.

They all trooped outside. More farewell kisses, handshakes, and hugs. Dad, fedora restored, held open the car door for his wife. Greg took Ruth's hand and opened the rear door for her.

She smiled weakly at him. "Thank you!" *Cheerful and charming*!

"My pleasure, ma'am. And keep drawing, Ruthie; keep sketching, keep painting!"

Settling on the back seat and closing her eyes, she hoped he would lean in and kiss her again. *Please kiss me again*. But she heard him step back. As they drove away, she had to make do with the memory of the one sweet kiss on her forehead.

X

"Let's have a look," Donna said, taking the postcard from Ruth. "What's this picture?"

"It's by Leonardo da Vinci. It's called the *Annunciation*."

"What does that mean?"

"Honestly, don't you know?" Jasmine sighed. "It's when the angel Gabriel arrives and tells Mary she's going to have a baby. Don't you learn nothin' at church?"

"'Course I do," Donna said unconvincingly. "Mary was Jesus' mom, and Gabriel was like the president of the angels. He sang to some shepherds at Christmas."

"Sort of," said Jasmine, again sighing. She adopted her thicker accent and added, "I don' know. When white man first met mah people *he* thought *we* was the heathens! I guess it's the other way around, really!"

"None of us are heathens," Donna said defensively, "I just find it boring. Anyway," turning the card over, "what does Ruth's boyfriend have to say?"

"He's not my boyfriend," Ruth protested feebly, secretly delighted. "You can both read it if you like."

Donna was already doing so. "It's nice," she said, handing it to Jasmine. "I wish I had an English boyfriend."

"He's *not* my boyfriend," Ruth repeated, even more delighted. *English boyfriend!* "I haven't got a boyfriend."

Morning school would soon begin, and a steady stream of

pupils were entering the building. The three girls were still on the bench beneath the oak tree, with Smokey the cat stretched out along his branch, tail dangling. Ruth, on arriving, had held up the postcard to show Smokey, but in the manner of cats he had twitched his tail, rubbed the side of his head against the branch, and ignored the *Annunciation*. Then Donna and Jasmine had arrived, and Ruth, excitedly waving the card at them instead, cried out, "From Greg! I've got a card from Greg!"

It had been waiting for her when she'd returned from school the previous day. Ten days had passed since Greg's departure. Ten long days during which she had alternated between intense euphoria at the very thought of Greg and replaying every moment of his presence, and intense anguish at his absence and the silence that stretched on forever. Every morning it had been, surely I'll hear from you today, a letter or a card – or will you even phone? Oh, that would be wonderful. Every afternoon arriving home from school it was, oh why haven't you written me? Have you forgotten me? You can't have forgotten me! Why haven't you written? Every night she headed for bed in a misery, which gave way to a warm feeling of joy as she looked at the Walden Pond drawing she had done of him – a true and telling likeness – which had ousted the multiple David Cassidys from her wall, and at the photos Uncle Harold had given her including, most preciously, the two of just her and the lopsidedly smiling Greg. She also had one of his erasers, which he had lent her on some occasion and not reclaimed, and her hardback notebook bought expressly for the purpose of recording memories of Greg and her hopes, joys and sadnesses about him.

And now she had this card! Only a brief message, addressing her as 'Ruthie', saying how much he had enjoyed meeting her, reminding her of the visit to Walden Pond – how could she forget! –

wishing her well with her art, and concluding with, 'see you again sometime. Much love, "Cousin" (!!) Greg xx'. Not just *love*, but *much* love! And the jokey reference to Mom expecting her on that first evening to call him Cousin Greg! And not just a single kiss, but two! Her cup, as she remembered Pastor Gravatt once exclaiming – though under rather different circumstances – runneth over.

Jasmine handed the precious card back to her. "You going to write him?"

"Yeah, I sure am." She tucked it back into her school bag where during the day she also kept the two photographs.

"What are you going to say?" Donna demanded. "Are you going to say, 'I'll love you forever and will you marry me when I grow up?'"

"Do you think I could?" Ruth said doubtfully.

"No! Don't be silly! But you could drop lots of hints that you hope to see him again *soon*. Say you're pining away, and he'll come running. Or flying."

"Stop teasing her," Jasmine said, but Ruth was thinking I could, couldn't I? She'd wanted to write immediately after he'd left, while he was still on his way back to England, but in the end had failed to do so. Not that she hadn't tried. Several times she had started a letter – but each time, after some variation of 'Dear Greg, I wanted to let you know how nice/lovely/wonderful it was to meet you, and to thank you for the time we did drawing together', she had seized up. What did she want to say? It had been impossible to know, so she had abandoned the letter, started it again later, and again seized up. But now his card had arrived she would write that evening, thanking him for the card, telling him a little of what Donna and Jasmine had said about the Leonardo picture, telling him what drawings she had been doing, telling him about the photographs Uncle Harold had given her. Or had he sent copies to Greg? And if so, what did Greg do with them? Look at them constantly, as she did? She would have to ask him something about drawing or art, so he would write back, and send her more 'much love xx'. She would sign her letter '"Cousin" (!!) Ruthie xx'.

*

That afternoon Miss Abrams, the school's part-time art teacher, took a class for Ruth's year. She was a rotund, enthusiastic young woman with short black hair and spectacles, which she was forever misplacing. During classes she wore an apron over her day clothes. Which apron varied from day to day, but always depicting a work of art: *Sunflowers*, *Mona Lisa*, *The Hay Wain*, *American Gothic*... Today it was, as she told them, *Woman with a Parasol*.

"No, Stephen," she responded to his facetious comment, "it's not an umbrella, it's a parasol. Now," she clapped her hands, "have you all brought in postcards or pictures or photographs, like I asked last time?"

Nearly all hadn't. Miss Abrams unzipped a large bag and tipped its contents onto a trestle table. Cards scattered across the surface, some of them tumbling to the floor. "Plenty to choose from here. Come up and sort through them, choose two or three you like, and let's see how you get on with copying one of them. Be imaginative! Be inventive! Stephen, don't do that, put it back on the table, please."

Ruth remained seated. She took from her bag the photograph showing her and a kneeling Greg with his arm round her waist and hers round his shoulders. His hair had flopped forward, and his eyes were wide open – adorably *very* Greg. She, on the other hand, had a smirk on her face, worryingly making her look a little like Brad. Well, in the sketch based on it she could change that to something more…more *sophisticated*.

While her classmates were still scrabbling through the pictorial outpourings on the table, Ruth collected a sheet of art paper from a pile on the table at the back, and a selection of charcoal sticks. As she returned to her table, Miss Abrams joined her.

"You've brought your own picture, Ruth? Well done. May I?" Without waiting for a reply, she picked up the photograph, then took her glasses from the top of her head and placed them on her nose. "Mmm. Good-looking young man. A brother?"

"Oh, no, no!" Ruth stuttered. "No. I haven't got a brother. He's a friend. A sort of relative who visited us. He's from England. And he's an artist."

"Even better! I wouldn't mind a relative like that! Right," returning the photograph, "I'll leave you to it, unless there's anything you want to ask? No? Charcoal today, I see? You might want to roll your sleeves up. I look forward to seeing the outcome. Now what is going on over there?"

Miss Abrams left Ruth and went to deal with some argument that had broken out involving Stephen. Ruth set to work. She liked drawing with charcoal, despite the ever-present possibility of smudges, and was soon absorbed in her task. Drawing as she always did with total concentration gave her a sense of peace, of somehow belonging to herself. Although – as she'd realized some time ago and puzzled over ever since – she never knew at the time that it happened, precisely because of that total concentration itself. Only afterwards, when her concentration on drawing or painting had ended and the rest of the world came rushing back in, did she realize, if she could have put it into words, how fully in harmony with herself she had been for the duration. But she didn't have the words: she didn't need them with the drawings, the paintings, the sketches. They were better than any words.

A jangle of voices, shouts and random noises of chair legs scraping on the floor and the banging of doors. Class, the last of the day, has ended. As the others pack up and head out in ones and twos and little groups, Ruth, still absorbed, is barely aware of the scrummage, only just registering but not responding to Donna's, "Bye-bye, sweetie pie!" then her starting to sing 'Could It Be Forever' before Jasmine shushes her, saying, "Stop it! Don't tease her! Bye, Ruth, see you tomorrow."

Miss Abrams' voice finally breaks through. "That's looking very good, Ruth, as ever," she says, "but you do need to finish now."

"Won't be a minute," Ruth murmurs, not looking up.

"The way you've just slightly changed the expression on your face – very well done. You really do have heaps of talent, don't you? You know the secret of making a few lines do so much. Shall I get you the fixer spray? It'd be a shame if this got smudged."

"Thank you!" Ruth smiles at Miss Abrams.

Fixer spray applied. Miss Abrams says she has some clearing up to do, and that when the fixer has dried she'll add the picture to Ruth's folder to store in the cupboard.

Ruth gathers her things and leaves. Miss Abrams thinks she has *heaps of talent*. Miss Abrams thinks Greg is *good-looking*. Greg has sent *much love* and *xx*. Miss Abrams thinks she has *heaps of talent*; Miss Abrams thinks Greg is *good-looking*; Greg has sent *much love* and *xx*. Miss Abrams thinks…

In an exultant mood on her way home, she convinces herself that Greg will be back in the States before long. She'll be a teenager by then. Does he know when her birthday is? Maybe not, but he could easily find out, couldn't he?

xi

Saturday May 18th. Ruth's birthday. She is now thirteen. A proper teenager at last.

The scent of wisteria, coming into bloom, is noticeable in the balloon-festooned hallway. The door has been propped open, and outside her dad is up the ladder again, attaching more birthday balloons to the trellis. A birthday cake awaits in the kitchen larder, and a birthday present from Mom and Dad is playing on the record player: a compilation of Beatles' singles. She is singing and dancing along to 'Please Please Me'.

Dad comes into the room, holding up the limp carcass of a red balloon. "*Pop* music," he says, miming puncturing it.

Wondering if he had deliberately burst the balloon to make the joke, Ruth blows him a kiss between verse and chorus, and carries on dancing as he returns outside.

The mail is late, but when it arrives there are, along with a healthy batch of cards, several parcels: from an uncle and aunt she rarely sees; from Mom's parents, Grandma and Grandpa; from Dad's father, Grandad; from Ted still away at college. Donna, Jasmine and a few other school friends will be coming round that afternoon for a party, as will Aunt Lou and Uncle Harold and Brad, bringing more cards and presents.

"There's this too," Mom says, holding out a flat parcel, all brown paper and adhesive tape, that she's been concealing behind her back. "It came a couple of days ago, so I kept it back for today. It's from England – see, that's their queen on the stamp!"

"Oh! Please! Please!"

Mom hands over the package with a little smile. Ruth tries to tear the paper off, but the tape is too tough.

"Scissors!" She dashes into the kitchen with the parcel and grabs them from their hook.

"Careful!" Mom has followed her in. "Don't cut yourself."

Ignoring her, Ruth slices through the tape and tears off the brown paper, dropping the bits on the floor. A padded envelope, unsealed. She tugs out a book along with two white envelopes. He's sent a birthday present! After his da Vinci postcard there's been nothing for nearly two months, despite the three chatty letters she's written him, and the lack of response has been so hard. Every night when she's gone to bed, she's gazed longingly at his photo and begged him to write her, begged him not to forget her. And he hasn't. He's found out her birthday and sent her a present!

She gives Mom the envelope addressed to George & Nancy, then tears open the envelope addressed to Ruthie. An agitated scan of the two sides of letter shows no reference to her birthday. So it's a coincidence that he's written her and sent the book now – but what a wonderful coincidence! *Thank you, God!* She'll read the letter properly in a minute after a quick look at the book. It's called *The Horse That Galloped Forever* by Anthony Fletcher, with – in a smaller typeface – illustrations by Gregory Adams. *Gregory Adams!* A children's storybook, containing Greg's drawings. She opens the book at the title page and can't stop her mouth dropping open. 'For Ruth', he has written. 'From one artist to a fellow artist! Love, Greg xx'.

"Gee, isn't that so kind," Mom says when Ruth shows her, and repeats her little smile. "He knows you're fond of him."

Ruth's eyesight goes blurry. She sniffs. A tear falls onto the book. She feels Mom putting an arm round her shoulders.

"That's just lovely of him, honey. Cheer up, I know you've been hoping to hear from him. Mothers can tell!"

"Mom! I'm not upset!" she manages to say through more tears and sniffs. "I'm really happy!"

"Well, why don't you go to your room and read that letter properly in peace! I know you must be longing to! And I'll see what he's got to say in my letter."

Propped up by two pillows, Ruth sits on her rumpled bedclothes to read the letter. It's not, despite her hopes, full of avowals of everlasting love, but is very friendly and easy. He admits that he is a 'rotten correspondent' but has enjoyed getting her letters. He warns her that the book is 'far too young' for her but hopes she won't feel insulted by it, as he thought she would like to see some of his pictures in print for the first time. She bites her lip and smiles. Of *course* she wants to see his pictures, almost as much as she wants to see him.

He writes how exciting it is for him to have his work appear in a book – 'I know people say that the art itself is what's important, not getting recognised for it. Which is true, but all the same it's jolly nice when you *do* get recognised even at a lowly level like this book, and it's given me quite a kick to have it published. I suppose,' he has added, 'a kick is just what a galloping horse would give!' He hopes she has been 'having a good time painting and drawing', and signs off with 'love, Greg xx', then adds a P.S.: 'I've sent more of my news to your Mum and Dad. Hope you approve!'

She returns to the kitchen where Mom is in the middle of sorting out crockery and cutlery for the party. "Mom, Greg says he's sent you some news. What is it?"

Mom wipes her hands on a cloth then pats her hair. "Let's go and sit down, honey."

"Why? What's the matter? Is he all right? Oh no!" Ruth claps a hand to her mouth in horror. "He's not been hurt, has he? He's not ill?"

"No, no. Nothing like that, honey. Let's go and sit down. Now, Ruth," when they're back in the main room, "I've got some news which is lovely for Greg, so I hope you'll be really happy for him."

"What is it? What is it?"

Already a dreadful suspicion has sprung up in her mind. The unimaginable.

"Greg says that he has just got engaged, and he's going to—"

Ruth lets out a long piercing wail. "No! No! Nooo!"

"Going to be married in a few—"

Ruth's wail intensifies.

"In a few months' time. He's sent a photograph of—"

But Ruth is no longer there. Still wailing, hands over her ears, she dashes out of the room, almost collides with her startled dad, and stumbles, sobbing, upstairs.

When her mom looks in on her ten minutes later, Ruth is lying face down on her bed, still crying. *How could you? How could you? Oh, I love you Greg, I love you!* She feels Mom sitting on the bed and placing a hand on her back. She twists round and sits up. "Oh, Mom! Oh, Mom!"

And Nancy Whitehead, like many a mother before her and many a mother since, clasps her broken-hearted sobbing daughter and rocks her as though she's a baby only a few weeks old.

*

Later, with Ruth still in her bedroom, weeping over Greg's photos and Greg's picture and the entries she has written in her Greg notebook, her dad comes in and sits on the bed.

"I'm so sorry, sweetheart."

Ruth continues to weep.

"Remember, we love you."

Ruth is not aware of when he leaves.

Downstairs, her mom is ringing around Ruth's friends and friends' parents, apologizing that the party has had to be cancelled because Ruth is not feeling very well. "No, nothing serious. She'll get over it soon, but she's had to retreat to bed. We'll let you know when we can reschedule the party…" "Thank you, Jasmine, I'll let her know you're praying for her, that's sweet of you…" "Thank you, Donna, maybe tomorrow, but give a ring first…"

It's only to her sister that she tells the truth.

"She'll get over it," Lou says reassuringly.

"I hope you're right. But how long will it take?"

"It took me about two weeks, I'd say! I can't remember. I don't think I noticed at the time. And you?"

"Quite a lot longer," Nancy Whitehead admits. "An entire summer at least for my real big one. I hope Ruth…" She sighs and does not finish the sentence.

xii

Summer came and went. Fall came and went. Christmas came and went. Changes in her body that her mom prepared her for had come. The brace on her teeth had gone.

Since the day of the terrible news, Ruth had written Greg twice. The first a day or two later – a result of her mom's insistence – was a card congratulating him on his engagement and wishing him and Penny – her usurper – 'all the very best wishes to you both for your future happiness. Love from Ruth'. Her words, hard to write, had been dictated by Mom. Then, about to seal the envelope, Mom busy with something else, Ruth had pulled the card out again, quickly changed 'Ruth' to 'Ruthie', adding 'I hope you won't forget me! x', thrust the card back into the envelope and stuck it down.

Her added plea did not bring a response.

The second occasion of her writing Greg had been several weeks later when she had decided to forgive him enough to send Xeroxes of several new drawings, thanks to Uncle Harold's state of the art machine. This time, after a week or two, he had replied, 'Hey Ruthie, Thanks for the pictures! They're really good. I very much like the dog looking up at Smokey. Great expressions on their faces! I'm very sorry to say, though, that some of the pix got damaged in the post – some idiot must have dropped the package in a puddle or something (the idiot wasn't me!). I can see you wrote "Donna" on the back – she's your "homecoming queen" friend, isn't she? And I particularly like the one of a young gypsy girl (is that what you call "women of the road" in the States?), but the water's made what you wrote on the back illegible. Hope you're all well on your side of the pond. Love, Greg xx'.

She had felt a mixture of pleasure that he'd written, relief that he hadn't mentioned *Penny* or whatever her name was, and annoyance that, whereas he had referred to the Donna picture, he had mistaken a self-portrait, based on a photo Uncle Harold had taken of her in a weird and wonderful costume for a school pageant, for *a woman of the road!* "Do I *look* like a young hobo?" she muttered crossly. Huh!

She was still feeling grumpy about it the next morning when Donna chided her, "You're in a mood. What's up?"

"What do you think?"

"Is it to do with Greg?" Jasmine said cautiously.

"He thinks I'm a hobo."

"He what?"

Ruth explained.

"He doesn't think you're a hobo!" Donna was laughing. "He obviously just didn't have his glasses on when he looked at your picture!"

"He doesn't wear glasses."

"Maybe he should start!" said Jasmine, also laughing.

"What it means," Ruth said, annoyed with her friends for laughing, "is that either I'm rotten at drawing, or he's rotten at remembering what I look like! Or am I just totally forgettable?"

"You're *brilliant* at drawing," Donna said. "You won that prize, and Miss Abrams put two of your pictures up in the school hall. Which means he must be rotten at remembering your... your..."

"Fair and lovely angelic features?" Jasmine suggested. "An' you sure ain't totally forgettable, hun!" in her self-parodying accent.

"Show us one of those photos you keep in your bag," Donna instructed, looking for something in her own bag. "You know, one of you and him. Come on."

"Why?"

"You'll see."

Puzzled, Ruth found and held up the first of the photographs.

"No, no. Turn it around. Look at your face in the photo, then at this." Donna had found and flipped open her compact, which she held up so that Ruth could see her own face in the mirror.

Her face in the photograph; her face in the mirror. She looked back and forth between the two images. "Well? What?"

"You're older now, that's what."

"Not much."

"But can't you see the difference? You're growing up! Like we all are."

"Specially at our age," Jasmine added.

"Oh." Ruth looked back and forth between the two images again. She couldn't, she had to admit to herself, see any difference; but all the same she knew what Donna and Jasmine meant. Growing up. Maybe she could feel it? Yes, yes, she could feel it must be so.

*

She had not written to Greg again, not even to tell him of winning a local schools' competition with her charcoal drawing of him. And although she still thought about him from time to time, usually with an upwelling of hurt and sadness, especially when in late November the news arrived, along with a number of incontrovertible photos, that he and Penny were now married, these moments grew increasingly infrequent.

The last communication from Greg had been after Christmas, when a belated card had arrived wishing Happy Christmas to George and Nancy – and Ruthie the artist. Greg's own work, it wittily depicted the hero of *The Horse That Galloped Forever* dressed up as a reindeer and harnessed to Santa's sledge. It made Ruth smile, and when the Christmas cards and decorations were taken down, she added it to her Greg memorabilia. It was the final item to be squirrelled away in the box, and birthday time had come round again when she next opened it.

xiii

Since her fourteenth birthday would fall on a Sunday, when there would be a little family gathering in the afternoon, she was going out Saturday evening with friends to celebrate. As she sat in her bedroom brushing her hair in readiness, she remembered her previous birthday, how her party had been cancelled all because of her crush on Greg.

She stopped brushing, went to her cupboard, and unearthed the small wickerwork box of mementos. For some while she gazed at the two photographs of her and Greg taken by Uncle Harold. "I look so young," she murmured to herself. "And you, you were very kind, but you are rather old for me, aren't you? Sorry, Greg, but I'm about to two-time you." She put the photos back in the box and the box back in the cupboard, then resumed brushing her hair. He had been nice of course, *really* nice, but how silly of her to have wanted his undivided attention. Donna had been right to tease her about it; and now it was *grossly* embarrassing to remember how she had thrown herself at him that final evening.

"Can I come in?" Her mom had come up the stairs.

"Sure."

"Oh, you look lovely, honey! Are you ready now for the finishing touches?"

Aunt Lou had given Ruth an early birthday present so she would have it in time for the evening out. A pouch of cosmetics, which Mom had promised to help her use.

"I'm not as good at this as Lou," Mom said, setting out the contents of the pouch on Ruth's dressing table, "but let's see how we go. Swivel around."

First a touch of lip gloss followed by a hint of eyeshadow, then, "I think we should forget about the mascara. Not quite suitable in my opinion. Save it for another occasion."

"I don't want to look like Morticia!"

"Some blusher, though. Hold still. You do have nice skin, Ruth, you know, and I do believe your freckles are really fading."

How *sweet* it was of Mom, Ruth thought, to be helping and not criticizing.

"That's all you need, honey," Mom said, stepping back to survey her handiwork. "Stand up. You're growing to be quite a beautiful swan, aren't you?"

Had she been an ugly duckling before, then? She smiled. Was that why Greg had told her she had an *interesting* face?

"Thank you, Mom!"

Mother and daughter hugged.

*

When the doorbell sounds, Ruth flies to the door, but Mom is already opening it. A group of her friends: Donna and Jasmine, Brad and his soccer-playing friend Tom, and Stephen, the *bad boy* of the class.

"Hi, Aunt Nancy!" Brad gives her a hug. "Hi, Ruth! Happy birthday for tomorrow! Hey, wow – you look neat! Give you a hug?"

They hug. Over the previous few months Brad has, for reasons she doesn't fully understand, become much more attentive, dropping his *Ruth-less* remarks and giving her these sorts of compliments. "He's sixteen now," Mom had commented on a previous occasion, without elaborating.

"You really do look great, birthday girl!" Donna cries. "Doesn't she?" she demands of Tom, taking his arm and shaking it. "Come on, say something!"

"You look really nice!" Tom mumbles to her shyly.

"Thank you!" Ruth smiles. "Um, I'll just get my coat."

Ruth collects her coat, which Tom, nudged by Donna, gallantly helps her put on. "Thanks, Tom," she says, even though his help had been more of a hindrance. "Bye, Mom."

Jasmine, Donna, Brad, and Stephen all follow suit in saying goodbye. Tom, head lowered, mumbles something that could have been anything.

"Have a good time, all of you," Mom says. "Remember, honey, what Dad said. If there's a problem with getting a cab back, you ring, and he'll come straight out. Understood?"

"Okay, yeah," Ruth says gaily.

Donna and Stephen go down the path followed by Jasmine and Brad. Ruth follows them feeling gloriously happy – she's going out on a *date*! – and, promising not to be late back, she's escorted by her bashful admirer, Tom, to the waiting cab.

And so it is that Ruth's crush would appear to have died, as crushes usually do. Hers seems to have left no scars, but in withdrawing it has deposited on the shoreline of her life just a wickerwork box of photos and other mementos, and her habitual use of *yeah* – a verbal fossil, as it were, forever speaking of a former age.

—*—

Afterword

In 1973, aged twenty-two, I visited my own 'distant relatives' in Massachusetts, having been best man at a friend's wedding in New York. And, yes, we joined up with another related family living nearby for outings such as to Concord and Walden Pond. They had a daughter of eleven or twelve ('Rachel', I will pseudonymously call her) who, the day before I was due to leave, flung herself on me, sobbing! This came right out of the blue, and was a little unnerving, but everyone, thank God, behaved kindly towards her (and though I regret to say I have no idea of what subsequently became of her, I'm confident she wouldn't have pined away for unrequited love).

A few years ago I read Aldous Huxley's 1955 novel *The Genius and the Goddess* in which a girl called Ruth, aged about fifteen, develops a crush on one of the male protagonists. He is cruel towards her: calling the poems she writes him 'lousy', and sneering at her attempts to use make-up. Curiously, I felt that Huxley himself had also been cruel by creating her in order, for the sake of the story, to be humiliated.

Perhaps weirdly, given that Huxley's Ruth was fictional, I wanted to redress the balance, and recalling my American experience of being the unwitting object of a young crush, I chose to write *These Years: 1973* to understand or, if not understand, to explore the 'story arc' of a crush. In doing so, naming my protagonist 'Ruth' acknowledges and, I hope, honours not only the real-life 'Rachel', but also Huxley's fictional character.

I expected it to be a stand-alone story, but it nagged at me to discover what subsequently happened to my fictional Ruth, so in due course her story will continue in *These Years: 1986*, and *These Years: 1991*.

Also by R N F Skinner from SilverWood

Still Crazy…

A dinner party. A cabaret.
The unforgotten past bursts into the present,
ripping open the future.

When Phil, an undergraduate at Cambridge University, performs in cabaret at a party, he meets and falls in love with Melanie. As she in turn appears to have fallen in love with him, he cannot understand why she then plays hard to get, even after he learns of the traumatic events that shaped her teenage years. But the influence of former boyfriend Simon is still strong, and she and Phil part. Twenty-five years later, both now married, they meet again by chance and resume their relationship. Soon each faces a tough choice: will Melanie decide on love or loyalty? Will Phil commit to his estranged wife or return to his first love?

"This is a wonderful novel, beautifully written, that threads its way through the lives and loves of its characters who step vividly out of the pages. A delight to read."
–The Rt Hon Lord Smith of Finsbury, Master of Pembroke College, Cambridge

ISBN 978-1-78132-991-7   RRP £11.99

After All…

Why have the Four Horsemen of the Apocalypse gone AWOL?
What exactly is the weird 'Armadillo Project'?
Who isn't cute in the Acute Medical Unit?

A collection of short stories and scripts, including The Lure of the Footlights featuring Phil, the male protagonist of Still Crazy…, before he meets Melanie. The scripts constitute a small selection of comedy sketches written and performed over many years, including 'Evans', the sketch with which the author gained membership of the Cambridge Footlights; 'Dead Safe', introducing the Health and Safety Officer of the Afterlife; 'Encountering Ourselves' with a dodgy group therapist; and the 'Steeplechase for Saints and Theologians' where St Paul and Thomas Aquinas compete with others to win a Crown of Glory.

"Great writing … [This] collection of stories and sketches is both profound and hilarious… I heartily recommend it."

–Dr Gordon R Clarke, author of 'Someone Else's Gods' (SilverWood 2022)

ISBN 978-1-80042-202-5   RRP £10.99

Milton Keynes UK
Ingram Content Group UK Ltd.
UKHW022050120524
442583UK00003B/79

9 781800 422759